Elfhame
Academy
Book 1

Tiffany Shand

ACKNOWLEDGMENTS

Cover Design by Creative Cover Book Designs

PROLOGUE

CASSIE

"Cassie, are you sure that girl is here?" My sister, Liv, asked me. She glanced around, uneasy. Her blue eyes looked dark under the dim streetlight and her lilac coloured hair almost white.

"This is the place I saw in my vision," I replied and shoved my long purple hair off my face. A streak of light darted overhead as my baby dragon, Murphy, shot through the warehouse.

"We need to find that girl so we can get Mum off the hook."

"We will, sis. Relax." I squeezed her arm. "Mum will be out of prison before you know it."

I still couldn't believe our adoptive mum/aunt had been arrested for helping a fugitive escape from custody. Our mum was straight as an arrow. Both in her old job as an enforcer and as a private investigator.

Up ahead stood the derelict warehouse. Its windows had long been broken out and now stood like empty eyes watching over us. Some of the roof had fallen away. The walls remained intact and loomed like silent sentinels. We headed through a gap on the side of the building where the door had fallen off its hinges.

The only way to get Mum out was to find the missing fugitive Lucy Grey. The whole thing still had my head reeling. A couple of hours ago I'd been off travelling through the elven realm of Elfhame. Until Liv called me back to help her out. It had taken me awhile to get up to speed on what happened. From the sounds of it Mum had been called to a local crime scene after an elf had been found dead and they had taken a suspect into custody.

Murphy zipped over our heads and waved his front paw to get my attention. His silver-grey scales shone like moonlight and his glowing amber eyes glowed like tiny balls of fire.

"How did you end up with that flying lizard?" Liv scowled at Murphy. "You never had him when you left a few weeks ago."

"I told you, I found him when I was in the mountains," I replied. "He was stuck on something, so I pulled him down." I didn't go into detail about telling her where I had really been as that would lead to unwanted questions. Questions we didn't have time for.

"Don't you think it's strange you found a dragon in the middle of nowhere? Why didn't you leave him there?"

I shrugged. I knew she'd ask questions, but the story of how I found Murphy would have to wait until later. "He kept following me. But he's good at finding and sensing things."

Come. Murphy's voice rang through my mind.

I hurried after him. Odd, I'd never heard him speak before. But I hadn't known him long enough to know what he could do.

"I can't believe we're following a dragon." Liv rolled her eyes. "Are you sure you can trust that thing? You don't know where he came from or —"

"Oh, come on." I grabbed her arm and dragged her along. "I know everything I need to know about him."

Up ahead stood another door.

Bad. Bad. Murphy skirted around the door.

The door had no handle or way to open it.

Liv stopped for a moment, using her empathic abilities. "I sense fear." She shivered. "She's in there. I can feel it."

"I'll get through it." I raised my hand and bright light flashed between my fingers. I threw a blast of purple light at the door and it burst open.

A brunette girl, who looked around seventeen, sat huddled in the corner. Most of her remained hidden by shadow.

Murphy circled around the girl, making his usual chirpy sounds.

"Please go away," Lucy said.

"No can do." I pulled out my cuffs. "You're coming with us."

"You don't understand. It's here. It will kill you both," Lucy cried. She looked up. Her blue eyes wide with fear.

"What will?" I frowned and twisted the cuff around her wrist.

"Cassie, something doesn't feel right." Liv turned pale. "We need to get her out of here."

Bad, bad. Murphy's voice rang through my mind again.

"Is there another shadowling here?" I asked.

Liv and I had already encountered a shadowling when we had searched the crime scene where the elven necromancer had been killed. Shadowlings were dark spirit that came out of the Nether Realm. I had fought one of them back in Elfhame when I'd found Murphy.

Liv and I glanced around, uneasy.

"We can't leave." Lucy pulled away before I had the chance to get the other cuff on her wrist. She ran away from us and out the door.

"Hey, come back here!" Liv yelled.

"Murphy, go get her!"

Murphy whizzed off in the opposite direction.

Liv and I raced after her. Something up ahead screeched and a black shadow raced across the wall.

Lucy stopped and turned white. "It's here."

"What's here?" Liv asked.

Light blinded me and an explosion ripped through the air. The blast slammed me against the wall and blackness swallowed me.

CHAPTER 1

CASSIE

Two months later

I clambered through the jarred and jagged remains of the warehouse. I'd been back almost every day in hopes of finding my missing sister. Of some trace of her, but I never did find anything. Liv'd disappeared that night and was now presumed dead. I'd woken up outside the warehouse with a concussion and ringing in my ears but no sign of Liv.

Murphy zigzagged above me. His silver-white scales shimmered like moonlight. He flew down and wrapped his tiny body around my shoulders. Weird. Once I would have scoffed at the idea of having a dragon sidekick. Now I couldn't imagine being without him.

I patted his head and he purred against me. Dragons purred like cats. Who knew?

I raised my hand, light flared between my fingers as I blasted more debris out of the way. More junk seemed to appear every day. The warehouse had been declared unsafe and condemned. Pretty soon there would be nothing left for me to search. No way would I believe Liv was dead, not until I had proof.

Maybe coming back here was a waste of time but this was the last place I'd seen my sister. It seemed like the only place where I would find any clues.

My phone buzzed. I pulled it out and Mum's image appeared on screen. Like me, she had long purple hair and pointed ears. Although her hair was lilac and mine dark purple. We both had azure blue eyes that hinted at our fae and elven heritage.

I groaned, then hit the button to answer the call. "Hi, Mum."

"Cassie, where are you?" she demanded. "It's the middle of the night. And I know you don't have any active cases at the moment."

"You don't know that. I don't tell you about every single case I'm working. Just like you don't tell me about some of your cases." The only bad thing about following in her footsteps and becoming a private investigator was she usually knew what kind of cases I worked. And when I worked them. "I'm out with Murphy. You know he gets antsy been stuck in the house." True enough.

Mum struggled with having a dragon around. Murphy struggled with it, too. Dragons weren't meant to be house pets. But I couldn't make Murphy leave — I'd tried already that and he either cried or came straight back.

"Please tell me you're not at the warehouse again."

Damn, she knew me better than I thought. Mum had searched for Liv as well but hadn't found anything either. That was what she had told me at least. She had scoured the warehouse, talked to the elven enforcers and human authorities. They ruled the explosion as suspicious and declared Liv dead. She seemed to have given up which puzzled me. How could she just give up finding Liv? It made no sense.

"Okay, I'm not at the warehouse again."

Mum gave a derisive snort. "Cassie, that whole place could come down on you. Come home. Right now. I told you to stop going there."

I rolled my eyes even though I knew she

What was this thing? I had grown up learning about different supernaturals and this didn't look like anything I'd heard of. Damn, so much for being clued up on different creatures.

Murphy shot out of my arms and opened his mouth. A plume of smoke came out. The creature roared again and advanced towards me.

I reached for my sword then realised I'd left it at home. Damn it. I started using my birth mum's sword around the time I'd discovered Murphy. It helped with fighting off all the weird things that started appearing since then.

I hit the creature with a blast of light. The creature stumbled but it didn't do much to deter him. I still had no idea why a spell to summon my sister would have bought that thing here. Nor did I have time to ponder the thought.

Murphy circled around the creature's head and scratched at him.

Think, Cassie.

Drawing more of my light, I hit him in the eyes. The creature screamed in agony. Grabbing a jagged piece of metal, I lunged for him. He blocked my arm and punched me hard. I reeled back and stars flashed across my vision.

He raised his hand to strike me again. Instead, I punched him so hard he staggered backwards. One good thing about being the daughter of the slayer was I had supernatural strength.

I punched him again, spun and kicked him in the stomach. The creature grunted. I knew I couldn't fight this thing forever. I had to get rid of it somehow. It lunged at me again.

On instinct, I raised my hands. Light burst from my palms and blasted the thing to the other end of the passageway.

I stared at my now-glowing hands. "What the hell?" My magic had never been this strong before.

If the spell had summoned the creature, maybe a spell would help get rid of it.

"Elements hear my call, remove this creature from these walls."

A tornado whipped through the building, knocking Murphy to the ground.

The creature screamed as the tornado whipped around it and spirited him away.

I stood on the spot for a few moments and half expected it to reappear. When nothing happened, I blew out a breath. Murphy flew over to me and I held him close. "What the hell just happened?" I ran a hand through my

CHAPTER 2

ASH

Unbelievable. I couldn't believe Cassie had just run off like that. Scrambling to my feet, I wiped blood from my hand from where her dragon had scratched me.

We were on the same side so I didn't know why she seemed so dead set with working against me. It made me wonder how Murphy could even survive here. I had been there when Cassie had found Murphy in Elfhame. So I wasn't surprised he had stayed with her. But dragons weren't known for staying in the human realm. This place didn't have enough magic to sustain them.

I guessed that was why Nina, Cassie's aunt and adoptive mother, had brought her to this realm. So she'd be safe from the monsters a slayer was supposed to destroy. We had been trained together as kids to get rid of the evil things that came out of the Nether Realm. I couldn't understand how she could just walk away from that. Being a slayer was who she was born to be and she was the last of her kind.

My phone buzzed and I answered it.

"Ash, why am I getting strong energy spikes from your location?" My boss, Cal, asked. "I've got a reading here that indicates a portal was opened. What in the nether's going on?"

"It's a long story. I had an encounter with Cassie again at the abandoned warehouse. Same place where Lucy Grey and Cassie's sister were attacked," I replied. "She wasn't too happy to see me. Do you think she can open portals now?"

"Open portals? Are you sure?" Cal sounded incredulous. "She's a slayer, not a magus."

She's your daughter, I wanted to say but didn't. I slipped my phone into my pocket and switched on my comm link on my ear. "Maybe she has more than slayer abilities."

"Did she tell you about what happened?"

"Not much. She doesn't seem to trust me anymore."

"Follow her. We need to know if she is

attracting things to the human realm. Bring her in if you have two."

I knew full well Cassie wouldn't be happy about that.

"I can't keep following her around like some kind of stalker. If I do, how am I ever going to gain her trust again?"

"You will if I make it an order. You're not her magus anymore or her friend. You need to remember that." Cal tapped away on a keyboard.

I continued running and scanned the area with my mind. Cassie and Murphy had vanished. "I'll look for her." I went to switch off my comm link. "Wait, she said something about finding her missing sister. Maybe that's why she's drawing energy here."

"Go after her and keep an eye on her. If she's attracting creatures from the Nether Realm, we've got a bigger problem than I first expected. But don't let her see you." Cal then cut the connection.

I took off the metal band that kept my other side under control. Long leathery wings slid out of my back. I took to the air. The glowing lights of Colchester spread before me in a riot of colour. Bright lights flashed past me. I never got to come to the human realm much. For the most part humans knew more about the fae than they did the elves.

Thanks to The Change humans knew fae and supernaturals were real. Just over twenty years ago parts of the fae realm had come into this one. So humans got up close with the fae. Some elves had come over during 'The Change)but they kept to themselves. Unlike the fae who integrated with humans. I never paid much attention to the ongoing feud between the fae and the elves. My job was as an enforcer and I had to make sure things from the Nether Realm stayed there.

How had Cassie summoned that thing with a spell? Let alone sent it away with a spell? That wasn't how slayer magic worked. Somehow I doubted the creature had been sent very far. She might have power, but she hadn't used the full extent of her abilities in years.

I flapped my wings and glided over the town. Below, I finally spotted a purple light darting through back alleys. That had to be Cassie and her dragon. I swooped lower, careful to avoid rooftops. I kept to the shadows and pulled my glamour in place so no one would see me.

She darted in and out of alleyways. Then doubled back a couple of times. Her dragon flew along beside her. Odd. Dragons weren't placid creatures. Murphy had become more attached to her than I'd expected. Maybe it was because he was still a hatchling.

I followed her until she stopped outside a house on Barrow Street. She glanced around, then took a running jump and leapt onto the first floor window. Lights shone on the ground floor so she had to be avoiding someone. It seemed like she wasn't opposed to using some of her slayer abilities. A slayer could move with speed and possessed supernatural strength.

She scrambled through the open window and Murphy flew in after her. She closed the window, I edged closer. I couldn't make out much of the room other than its lilac coloured walls. Clothes were strewn across the floor and books and paperwork lay haphazardly over a messy desk.

"Cassie, where the hell have you been?" someone shouted.

I flew closer and spotted another woman. Her aunt Nina, who she now referred to as her adoptive mother. She had long lilac coloured hair and pointed ears. Nina Morgan was a fae PI and former investigator. I would recognise her anywhere. Nina clashed with the elves frequently and with my boss. Cal wouldn't be happy to learn about her involvement.

"Mum, I was… Just out with Murphy. You know how he hates being cooped up," Cassie said, trying to play innocent.

"I've already lost your sister. I'm not about to lose you too," Nina said. "You need to stop going back to that warehouse. There's nothing there to find."

"I'm not going to die, Mum. All I did was go back to the warehouse," Cassie said.

Nina ran a hand through her hair. "There's nothing in the warehouse but an unstable structure. You're lucky the whole place didn't come down on you."

Cassie glared at her aunt. "At least I'm doing something to find Liv, unlike you. You seem more focused on other cases than finding her!"

"That's not true," Nina said. "Did you find anything?" Nina pinched the bridge of her nose.

"Nothing on Liv. A weird creature attacked me," Cassie said. "And Ash showed up again. I can't believe the bloody elves of following me around!"

Nina put a hand over her eyes. "Oh, good goddess. What was the creature? Are you hurt?"

"No, and I've no idea what it was. Look

pretty burned up to me but I got rid of it. "

"Cassie, you can't keep using magic irresponsibly like this. There are dangerous things coming through from the Nether Realm. You'll attract them if you keep meddling in things you shouldn't be messing with."

"I think we both know why they're coming after me." Cassie crossed her arms.

"Because of that damned dragon you brought home, no doubt. I told you to take him back to elven realm."

I shook my head. I couldn't believe Nina would think Murphy would attract such creatures. She was using that dragon as a lame excuse.

"Stop looking for your sister. You're not going to find anything."

Interesting. I hadn't expected Nina to have given up searching for her niece so easily. Did she agree with the elves that Olivia had been killed the night of the explosion? We might not have found a body, but the investigators had ruled out the chances of anyone surviving the explosion.

Cassie's eyes widened with a look of hurt. "How can you just give up? Murphy isn't going anywhere. Now get out!" Cassie hugged the dragon and he rested his head against her chest.

"I don't want to give up. I've looked everywhere for your sister and there's no trace of her. That means she's not coming back. As much as I miss her, we can't waste our lives looking for her when there's nothing left to find. You've read the reports. You know there couldn't —

"No! She's not dead. If you think that then get the hell out!"

"Cassie —"

"I mean it, go away!"

Nina sighed and headed out of the room.

Odd. From what I remembered of Nina she never walked away from a fight.

Cassie slammed the door shut and wiped tears off her face.

I watched her while I landed on the neighbour's roof. No way would I land on Cassie's house and risk triggering Nina's security.

Tomorrow Cassie and I would have to have a chat with Cal and decide our next course of action.

CHAPTER 3

CASSIE

I rolled over in bed the next morning and groaned. A crack of light came in through the curtains but the weird feeling of being watched had gone away. Looking around last night hadn't revealed anyone. I knew Ash or one of the Elhanan was probably watching me.

Next time I went out I'd borrow Mum's car if she didn't need it. Transportation potions were expensive and I planned on going back to the warehouse later.

When I out onto the landing, I found a note on the table.

Had to pop out to work on some case stuff. Be back soon, Mum xx

That wasn't unusual. Mum could be called away at all hours of the day or night. I'd grown used to it over the years.

My heart sank. I wanted to talk to her and convince her not to give up on Liv. But I knew she had to work. Feeding a baby dragon proved more expensive than I'd imagined. I hadn't worked for a few months either due to travelling. I had saved up money so I could buy passage into Elfhame. That had been expensive as had moving around the elven realm. The elves had border guards in every province and they had been suspicious of a young woman travelling alone. Coming home would have been a nightmare with Murphy in tow. Luckily, Mum's reaper friend, Lily, transported me and Murphy back.

Heading downstairs with Murphy, I carried my laptop and my birth mother's sword with me. After the attack last night, I didn't want to be caught off-guard again.

I shoved some bread into the toaster and gave Murphy his usual meat. Propping the sword up, I sat at the kitchen table with my laptop. Bright sunlight poured in through the kitchen window, making the wooden cupboards and the whitewashed walls look brighter than they really were.

"We've got to find a better way to get you food, Murphy. The good stuff's too pricey. Maybe it's time I start taking on some cases of my own again."

I had money saved up but I didn't want to tap into that unless I had to. I wanted to focus on finding my sister but that wouldn't pay the bills. Maybe it was time to look for somewhere else to live and work as well. There were plenty of places around Colchester that I could rent out and live in. So I could do a few side jobs here and there to pay for stuff and keep Murphy well-fed.

Murphy wolfed his steak down in one go.

Tapping away on my laptop, I dug into the places where I knew Mum kept her files. I didn't know why she bothered hiding stuff from me anymore. One way or another I always found things. My toast popped up from the toaster and I nibbled on it. Mum hiding stuff from me, especially case files, had become a fun challenge between us over the years. But now it just irritated me. This was my sister. Murphy jumped onto the table. He grabbed my other piece of toast in one fell swoop.

"You sneaky bugger!" I laughed, then turned my attention back to the laptop. Nothing appeared on screen unless she had cleverly disguised something with different file names — something she frequently tried to do.

I knew I would probably have to do some digging around for it. I hadn't had any luck getting into the Elhanan's database to see what case files they had either. I did manage to pull up Ash's record, though. Which hadn't been easy. From what I'd read, he spent time working in the elven army before joining the enforcers. I couldn't find out much else about him though. Everything else was covered behind layers of security.

I flipped through Mum's open case files. Two adultery cases and one human who'd skipped bail. Even though I had my PI licence it didn't feel enough for me. Mum had her calling. Liv worked in the music industry for a while until that had soured. Over the past few months she had been working at our aunt's nightclub on Elfhame Academy Island. It wasn't easy getting onto the academy's island unless you were a student or worked there as an enforcer. I hadn't managed to get onto the island because the enforcers had blocked me at every turn. They had allowed Mum through only once.

The elves did like to keep to themselves. Maybe my ex, Mike, could help me in getting into the elven enforcers' case files. He was a complete nerd who was good at breaking into protected databases. I'd call him later to see if he could help me out.

I typed in another search with different keywords. Mum thought she was good at hiding things but I knew better. Finally some case files appeared. I clicked on them and opened each one. My eyes roamed over the screen as I took in details from her notes, files from the human police force and reports she had from the Elhanan.

Everything on there concluded the explosion had been caused by unstable magic within the warehouse. So far no one had managed to identify what had been used. All of the reports said substance/magic unknown. That made no sense either.

I scoured through more of the Elhanan's report. Most of it sounded vague with no real answers. They didn't even mention who they had ruled as being Jared's killer. News reports had stated Liv had been involved and must have killed him. That pissed me off. My sister wasn't a killer and that didn't explain the explosion. Liv couldn't have done that either.

Glass smashed as something burst through the patio doors in the living room. The house alarm screeched, almost deafening me. The creature from last night roared as it stormed into the kitchen and lunged straight towards me.

Holy crap! How the heck did that thing come back? Or find me for that matter?

Murphy shot into the air and blew smoke into the creature's face.

I grabbed my sword and slashed it. The blade flashed with light. Sure, I hadn't used a sword very much since I was a kid but I still remembered how to use one. I dodged its next swipe. Somehow I had to get rid of this thing.

The creature swiped me again. I lashed out with the sword. "I wish you'd go away," I snapped and blasted it with light again.

The creature staggered, then lunged forward and grabbed my sword. I yanked the blade away and slashed at it. If I got this out of this, I'd make sure I got some more practice in with the sword. At least then I wouldn't be so rusty.

The creature continued to thrash and lunge at me.

I jumped onto the kitchen table and kicked it in the head. The force of the blow slammed the creature across the room. Good thing I still had my slayer strength.

The alarm continued to wail which set my teeth on edge.

Think. How can I get rid of this?

"Demon who has come here, I call on you

to disappear," I chanted.

Light flashed around the beast but it didn't make it disappear. Useless bloody spell! But it was hard to come up with a decent rhyme in the middle of a battle with the blaring alarm going.

Murphy latched onto the creature's head and clawed at him.

I ran into the living room where I knew Mum kept a weapon hidden. If my sword couldn't deal with this thing, maybe a stunner would. Several thousand volts of electricity might do it some good.

The creature roared and stomped after me. With Murphy still thrashing at it.

Fumbling, I felt around in the cabinet for the stunner.

The creature knocked Murphy away so hard Murphy hit the wall. Murphy slid down the wall and landed in a heap, unmoving.

"Murph. Murph, are you okay?" I forgot all about the stunner.

No one hurt my dragon! Something inside me snapped. Power rose through me like an oncoming storm. Light flared between my hands, brighter than I'd ever seen before. I blasted the creature. The light tore through his body. I wanted it dead. I wanted it gone.

The wail of the alarm faded as the sound of

screaming echoed through my ears and the sound of more things breaking. Light blinded me as I found myself in a darkened room with shadows dancing against the walls in the pale moonlight.

I blinked and found myself back in my living room and didn't have time to ponder what the hell just happened. I dodged the creature's next blow, kicked it away from me and let my purple light flow free. All of my bottled emotions came out. I had lost my sister and now Murphy had been hurt. I was sick of losing people. Sick of things coming after me.

The creature screamed as my light tore it apart until nothing remained. Light exploded through the living room in a burst of purple orbs.

I stood and stared at the spot. Then I looked at my hands. I killed that thing. Shouldn't I feel something? Relief? Anger? Something?

Instead, numbness washed over me.

Light continued to pulse over my hands. What had changed? Had my powers grown?

Where hell had that screaming come from? It hadn't felt like a vision or had it been one? No, I knew visions when I saw them. Besides, that ability was too unreliable to show me things very often. I could go months without seeing anything.

The back door opened and someone rushed into the room. Ash along with another man.

Ash wore his usual dark jeans and leather jacket. The second man was another powerfully built elf with tanned, short dark hair and silver eyes. He wore a short trench coat and what looked like a suit underneath.

"Cassie, what did you do?" the other man asked. "Where is the baneling?"

Oh wonderful, it just had to be my father.

I didn't respond. I still felt too numb to say anything. Had what I'd seen and heard even been real? If so, when had it happened? It felt familiar to me somehow. Almost like a memory from a dream.

"Cassie, are you okay?" Ash took my hand and the light fizzled out. "Did the baneling hurt you?"

"Where's your dragon?" Cal asked.

That brought me to my senses and I remembered what had happened. "Murphy!" I shot over to him and fell to my knees. "Murph, please wake up." I picked him up in my arms. "Come on, Murph." Murphy whined and opened his eyes, then sprang into the air. "Oh, thank the goddess." I cuddled him close and stared at the two elves. "What are you doing here?" I couldn't believe they had come into my home now.

"We were on our way to come and talk to you," Cal answered. "I think you know why we're here. The Elhanan—"

The Elhanan or the elves' version of enforcers. I never liked them since they seemed to have covered up my sister's disappearance and named her as a murderer.

"Why? Why would I want to see you?" I glowered at him.

I hadn't wanted to see my father after my birth mum had been killed and hoped I would never see him again. The first time I'd seen him in over seven years had been after Lucy Grey had been arrested a few weeks ago but we hadn't conversed much then.

"Did you kill the creature or did you send it away like last night?" Ash asked.

"I killed it. Are you following me around now?" I put my hands on my hips. My feeling of being watched must have been real. Had they been watching me since last night? Bloody cheek!

"We had to. It's not every day we find someone who can summon things from the Nether Realm."

"Cassie!" The front door burst open, the

alarm finally went silent and Mum rushed into the living room. All colour drained from her face. "Cal, what the fuck are you doing here?"

"Shall we sit down and discuss this?" Cal suggested. "We all have questions, I'm sure."

"No. I want you out of my house." Mum glowered at him and stepped over to me. "Cassie, are you alright?"

I shook my head. "I think so. The enforcers were just leaving."

"Get out, both of you." Mum motioned to the door. "Your kind aren't welcome in my house. Especially not a former magus." She spat out the word *magus*.

"Nina, you know we can't leave. Cassie has a lot of power," Cal said. "She summoned a baneling and killed it."

"I want you out now. My daughter isn't an elf. You have no authority here."

"If you don't hear us out, I'll take Cassie into custody," Cal stated. "So it's in your best interest to listen to us."

"Fine, talk." I crossed my arms. "But I'm not going anywhere with you."

CHAPTER 4

CASSIE

The four of us sat at the dining room table. I went off to the kitchen to make some tea. Not for them but for Mum and me. Broken glass and other debris littered the floor. I waved my hand and levitated everything into the bin. We'd have to board up the patio doors in the living room later.

But in the end I changed my mind, poured two mugs and doused them with truth potion. Expensive stuff, but this seemed like a necessary situation. Mum always kept some in the house in case she ever needed it. Ash might have been my friend once, but I didn't know if I could trust him anymore. And I'd never trust my father.

I considered adding something stronger to my tea but didn't. I'd need a clear head for this.

No sound came from the dining room. Mum sat and glared at them when I came in with the tea.

"So, Cal, tell us why you're in my house," Mum growled. Odd. She never usually lost her cool in front of anyone. But she'd never been a fan of my father either.

"Last night we were doing our usual sweep of creatures that come through from the nether," Cal said. "Ash was in the area and we got some strong energy readings from a derelict warehouse. The same warehouse where your niece was recently killed."

I slammed the tray of tea down. Hot liquid sloshed over the table. "My sister isn't dead. She's missing," I snapped. "No thanks to you arseholes who covered up her disappearance and named her a murderer."

"Your sister —" Cal closed his mouth and paused. "That case has been closed. But we have more important issues to deal with."

"What did you do last night?" Ash asked me. "Talk us through everything that happened."

I slumped into a chair beside Mum. "I went to look for signs of my missing sister. Seeing as no one else is bothering to look for her. Why?"

"You performed magic, yes?" Cal arched a brow. "Also, there's no way your sister could have —"

I cut him off, "My sister is alive and no one will convince me otherwise. And yeah, I cast a spell to summon her. Then that weird creature appeared."

"That's the baneling." Cal nodded. "What kind of wording did you use in the spell? Did you just chant something or use runes?"

I narrowed my eyes. "What's it to you? I'm fae, not elf. What magic I use isn't your business. You don't even have jurisdiction here."

Cal's lips twitched. "Your mother may have had fae and witch blood but she was an elf slayer and I am a full elf. So you are —"

"Please don't remind me of that. I'm not a slayer. I walked away from that."

"But you can't deny your heritage. It's who you are. It's what your mother wanted you to be."

That sounded so ridiculous I almost laughed. He dared to have the audacity to come here and tell me what my birthmother would have wanted.

Mum snorted beside me. "Don't pretend to know what Estelle would want for her daughter. Some magus you were. You let her die."

I flinched at that. "If you've come here to convince me to be the slayer, don't bother. Both of you can leave right now."

"It's our duty to monitor everything that comes from the Nether Realm. Just as it's yours to help us get rid of it."

"I didn't summon that thing. Hell, I got rid of it," I retorted. "You're welcome by the way."

"My daughter's lineage isn't your business. She's fae, not elf. As far as anyone is concerned, you aren't even her father," Mum insisted. "You aren't even listed on her birth record."

That didn't surprise me. My birthmother had had a forbidden relationship with Cal so she wouldn't have wanted anyone else to find out about who my father was. Especially not the elves themselves.

"Cassie, you have a lot of power. It's almost impossible for someone to summon a nether creature to the human realm," Cal remarked. "Now you're of age your powers have grown. Which means you can't hide away in the human realm like you did when you were a child."

"You're stronger than any elf I've met." Ash frowned at his tea. "There's truth potion

41

in this." He pushed the mug away.

Damn. I should have known I wouldn't get anything past him. Now I would have no way of knowing if they had told me the truth or not. Mum narrowed her eyes at me at the mention of the truth potion but she didn't say anything. Hell, she would probably have tried the same thing if she'd been given the chance.

"Even if I did summon something, so what?" I crossed my arms. "It was an accident."

"Your powers are growing stronger. Ash noticed that when he met you in Elfhame a couple of months ago. That makes you dangerous. Since you are my daughter —"

If he said that one more time I would hit him.

"My life and my powers aren't any of your damn business. Don't play the daughter card with me. You've never been my father."

Something passed across Cal's face but I couldn't name the emotion.

"Agreed. You're not welcome here so get the hell out of my house," Mum snapped.

Murphy landed on the table; sniffed Cal's mug then lapped at the tea in mine.

"Like it or not I can't leave, your powers are attracting unwanted attention. Since you have elven blood it's my duty to make sure you're not a danger to anyone in this realm or in any other realm. It's also unusual you have a dragon." Cal motioned to Murphy. "Dragons aren't pets. You can't keep him here."

I put a protective arm around Murphy. "He's none of your business either. Don't you dare try and take him away from me."

I knew how elves worked. If they found out Murphy came from Elfhame, they would take him away. They'd use the excuse of him being from the elven realm. How much had Ash told Cal about me?

"Cassie, it's in your best interest to cooperate with us," Cal said. "If you don't get your powers under control, you'll —"

"I've had enough of this." Mum shot to her feet. "You're both done asking questions. You can't take her in for misuse of magic. She can't have summoned the baneling."

"Nina —" Cal protested.

"Enough, Cal, maybe I should remind your precious bosses how you let my sister die."

A shadow passed over Cal's face. "That —"

Light flashed and a glowing piece of paper appeared on the table.

"I'm afraid you won't have any choice but to answer questions now," Cal remarked.

Ash muttered a curse. "How did they find out so fast?"

The letter had my name on it so I picked it up and opened it. "Cassandra Morgan, you are hereby summoned by the elven high council. Come to the citadel at twelve PM today. Failure to do so will mean you will be brought in by force." I scowled. "How do they even know about me?"

No one bothered to answer my question. Looked like I had no choice but to talk to the elves after all.

Mum told me to leave the room for a while so she could talk to Cal in private. Although I could hear her shouting at him.

I couldn't believe I'd been summoned by the Elven Council. I was fae for crying out loud. I also had witch blood. That didn't make me elven just because of who my mum's sperm donor had been.

I stayed with Ash in the living room. Broken glass to lay on the floor from where the baneling broke in. Scorch marks covered the cream-coloured walls and part of the plush cream rug in front of our stone fireplace had been burned from my magic.

"So is that your job now? Spying on me?" I demanded. "I can't believe you told him about me or about Murphy. I thought you were of my friend."

"I am your friend, Cas. But I still have a job to do and I can't ignore that."

I scoffed. "You haven't been my friend for a long time, Ash, so don't pretend to be one now. Why do you have to be here?" I scowled at him.

He leaned against the wall and crossed his arms. "Until you're presented to the council, yeah."

"Don't see why I need to see the council," I grumbled. "I'm not an elf even if I look like one. I haven't done anything wrong."

"Cas, your powers are growing. You can't deny the fact you're a slayer."

"I'm not walking back into that life. I've lost enough already. I'm not a danger to anyone and you're an idiot to think I am."

"Monsters are being drawn here because of your power."

I snorted. "Monsters aren't drawn to me. They're drawn to you. Isn't it your job to get rid of them? You're the enforcer."

The Elhanan were a secretive bunch. They kept to themselves and hunted monsters and worked as enforcers for the Elven Council. I knew of them because of the work my family had done and encounters they had with them over the years. Mum always said they were a nightmare to deal with.

He shook his head. "Your powers are like a beacon. I can feel it. And you have Murphy." Murphy perched on top of the fireplace and stared at Ash. He flew over and sniffed at him then huffed in a happy way. "Hi, there." Ash gave a genuine smile then touched Murphy's head. "It's good to see you again."

Traitor, I thought and said, *Murphy, we don't like him. You should bite him. He's not our friend.*

Murphy ignored me and enjoyed Ash's attention.

I gritted my teeth and flipped open my laptop. "What happens after I see your stupid council? You can't force me to be the slayer."

"That's up to the council to decide. They'll probably want to test your abilities."

"I already know what my abilities are. If they view me as a threat, they can't get rid of me like they did with my sister." I had no way of proving if the Elhanan were involved in Liv's disappearance but it wouldn't surprise me.

"They wouldn't have done anything to your sister. That's not the way we work."

I scoffed at that. "Yeah right."

The arguing grew louder.

"You let my sister die!" Mum yelled. "You

46

were supposed to protect her! Theres no way I'm letting you drag Cassie into danger!"

I really needed to talk to Mum. Closing my laptop, I headed into the dining room. Seeing Cal again had really riled her up.

What was the big deal? My birth mum's death was supposed to have been solved years ago. Mum should have been more upset over Liv's disappearance. Not her dead sister.

"You. Leave us," I told Cal. "Mum and I need to talk before we leave." To my surprise, Mum had tears in her eyes. "You leave too," I told Ash and yanked Murphy away from him.

They both went outside much to my relief. "Mum, what the hell is going on? Why are you going on about my birth mum?"

"It's — it's complicated, Cassie." Mum sniffed and wiped her eyes. "I shouldn't have let my emotions get the best of me. Cal being here brought up a lot of history."

"Well, make it less complicated." I crossed my arms. "What's going on with you?"

She wiped her eyes. "Seeing that… Man again. It brings back so many bad memories of when I lost my sister. Having them blame Liv for that elf's death just makes it worse."

"Don't tell me you believe you've killed that elf? Because we both know that's ridiculous."

47

Mum sniffed. "Of course I don't believe that."

"Then why have you given up on her? How can you just believe she's dead?"

"Don't you think if she was out there she would have contacted us by now? I did my own tests from what they found in that warehouse. No one could have survived the explosion. It's a miracle you got out of there alive. That's why you need to leave this alone before you get yourself killed." Her hands clenched into fists.

I shook my head both in disbelief and to clear it. "Why didn't you tell me this before? You're the ones walking around pretending like nothing happened."

"You want me to fall apart? Because I'm hanging on by a thread as it is!"

"I won't give up on her. I never will. If you've given up, that's your problem. But I'll do anything I damn well can to find out what happened to her." I turned to leave, unable to look at her anymore. "Why do I have to go before the council? They can't force me to be the slayer, can they?"

"I don't think so, no." She shook her head. "But if they view you as a threat... Don't worry, I'll take care of this."

"Maybe we should call Grandma." If I

knew my grandmother, she would know how to handle something like this.

"Good goddess, no. The last thing we need is for her to be there."

"Nina, it's time to go." Cal stuck his head through the back door.

I groaned. Why couldn't I have more time? I needed to know what else Mum knew. Pulling my phone out of my pocket, I send a quick text. Once I went before the council the shit would really hit the fan.

But I had to see this through or I would have an even worse fate.

CHAPTER 5

ASH

I stayed close to Cassie and her mother as we escorted them to Elfhame. We took them to a local spell circle to transport there. A circle owned by the fae but as enforcers they allowed Cal and I through.

A few moments later, we reappeared in the palace in Elfhame.

"This is just an informal meeting," Cal reassured them. "There's nothing to worry about."

I wouldn't be so sure of that. The Elven Council didn't like potential threats and Cassie would be that to them. Most of the elves weren't big fans of the slayer either. Despite her prickly nature, she had a strength about her. She looked like she had been through some shit in her life but survived it.

We led them through the sweeping marble hallways that were covered with plants and ornate statues. Being at the palace always made me uncomfortable. I hated elven nobility. They looked down on me as much as the fae since I was mixed raced and looked like a dark elf. But old prejudices would probably never die.

How did the council find out about her? I asked Cal in thought. *We never told anyone about Cassie.*

He shook his head. *No idea. I thought we kept our search under the radar.*

Someone in the tower must have seen our searches. I cursed.

"What happens when I meet the council?" Cassie bit her lip.

"I'm not sure what they know about you. They will ask you questions and perhaps perform a test," Cal answered. "You have nothing to worry about."

Cassie snorted. "I always worry when elves are involved. Nothing good ever comes from you."

We led them to a small waiting room.

"Stay here until you are summoned," Cal told them.

Cassie and Nina headed inside. We remained in the hallway.

"Nothing to worry about?" I scoffed. "You

know how the council treats threats. They eliminate them. She's still a kid."

"She's nineteen and of age under our laws."

"Since Cassie is elven, why not send her to the academy? At least there I could train with her again."

Cal furrowed his brow. "She could benefit from the academy, but I doubt she would agree to go there. We could benefit even more from her abilities at the Elhanan."

My eyes widened. "You want her to join us?" I snorted. "I doubt she'll ever agree to that. Especially given the way she feels about us."

"We'll keep that option open. Better that than the council locking her up or worse." He grimaced.

I leaned back against the wall. "You wouldn't let that happen, would you? She's your daughter and she's the slayer."

Keep your voice down and don't mention that fact around here, Cal warned. "I'm being summoned." Cal sighed. "Keep an eye on them." He stalked off down the hall.

I pressed my hand against the wall so I could listen in on what Cassie and Nina said.

"What are you hiding about my mum's murder?" Cassie snapped. "Is her case not closed?"

"Cassie, we can't talk about this here. And yes, the case is closed. Why are you even bringing that up?"

"Because I've never seen you act so riled up around someone like you did with Cal. You told me never to ask questions about my birth mum's death. Why is that?"

I frowned and pulled out my phone. I did a quick search for Nina's sister. But nothing appeared. Why wasn't there any matching for Cassie's birth mum? There should be some record of the slayer. It made no sense for there not to be. Cal had not only had a personal relationship with her but had been her magus. Why wouldn't he have files on her? Did he have something to hide?

I made a mental note to dig deeper into the Elhanan's files later. They should have had something on her. Slayers had once been an integral part of elven society. Not all the elves liked the slayer but they still needed one.

Cassie and Nina fell silent.

Nina had done something to block me out. I probed the room deeper with my senses until I heard them again.

"... Whatever happens you just tell them you're fae," Nina instructed. "Don't talk about your mother or what she was."

I didn't understand why they wanted to

keep Cassie's slayer heritage a secret. I can deny what she wants. Just because Nina had changed Cassie's surname

Cal returned a few moments later and headed straight into the waiting room. "It's time to go."

We headed for the council's main meeting room. Flags fluttered overhead depicting symbols for each of the noble elven families. The oak walls shone with rich tapestries of castles and forests. On the tiled floor loom so bright I could almost see my reflection in it.

The four council leaders. Katya, Mordora, Tyrone and Luis sat at the head of the room. Two sentinels stood nearby clutching staff weapons up. Both blond, muscular elves. The pride of the Queen's Guard.

Cal led Cassie up to a small podium where she had to sit, Nina and I sat in chairs in the empty stand.

"I present Cassandra Morgan before the council," Cal announced and bowed his head to the council leaders before he retreated to the other side of the room to join me and Nina.

Murphy wrapped himself around Cassie's shoulders.

"Do you know why you're here, child?"

Tyrone asked. Unlike the others, he had short auburn hair that rose in a mop of unruly curls. He didn't have the same kind of muscle as the sentinels. Instead, his body showed signs of a pampered life and he had dark green eyes.

"No. They said I somehow summoned something from your Nether Realm."

"Our Nether Realm?" Katya laughed. She pushed her long wavy blond hair of her face and her blue eyes widened. "The Nether Realm belongs to no one. It's nothing more than a wasteland. Did you summon the baneling on purpose?" She wore a long navy-blue velvet dress. Some of the elder ~~the~~ elves refused to adopt a more modern clothing. Even the sentinels had leather armour on and held weapons as if they were about to run off into battle.

"I didn't summon anything. Not on purpose anyway. So I don't see why I need to be here." She leaned back in her seat and crossed her arms.

I bit back a smile. She had tenacity; I'd give her that.

The eyes of all four council leaders widened.

"We'll be the judge of that." Tyrone leaned forward in his seat. "What were you doing at the warehouse yesterday?" He glanced at his tablet. "Do you often visit derelict warehouses in the middle of the night?"

Cassie's jaw tightened. "I went there to trace my missing sister. You must know about the explosion that happened there."

"Indeed, but your sister has been declared dead by the fae and human authorities," Mordora spoke up. She had birdlike features and flaming red hair.

"My sister isn't dead. If she were, there would be some trace left." Cassie went on to explain how she cast a summoning spell and how the baneling appeared. She recited the words to the spell.

Odd. I was no expert but that sounded like a pretty specific spell since she'd used her sister's name.

"I fought the baneling and sent it away with another spell. It came back and attacked me at home this morning," Cassie went on. "I got rid of it. Case closed."

"Banelings aren't known for their tracking skills," Luis remarked. "How did it find you?" He had short sandy blond hair and a willowy figure.

Cassie shrugged. "How should I know? I didn't even know what it was until they told me." She threw a glare at me and Cal. "If things are coming out of the Nether Realm, that's your problem not mine."

"So you used careless magic?" Katya arched an eyebrow. "I thought your mother would have taught you better than that given who she is." She threw Nina an annoyed look. "Or is there something you're hiding from us?"

Nina flinched beside me.

What she so afraid of? I couldn't see a problem with Cassie becoming the slayer again.

"What's your lineage? Who are your parents?" Tyrone asked. "Your record states you had a closed adoption and the records have been sealed — even from us. That's unusual given you were adopted at twelve years old."

Cassie bit her lip and didn't answer.

He turned his attention to Nina. "Why are her records sealed?"

"Because the adoption was private." Nina gritted her teeth. "I'm fae and not subject to your laws." She shot to her feet and strode across the room towards Cassie. "This is ridiculous. We all agree no harm was done last night. Creatures coming out of the Nether Realm is your problem, not ours. So we'll be leaving."

"Not yet, Miss Morgan. We haven't

decided whether your daughter is a threat or not." Katya held up a hand. "Until we do, you're not going anywhere."

So Nina kept Cassie's adoption a secret from the elven authorities. Clearly she had wanted to hide the fact Cassie was the daughter of the former elf slayer.

Why was Nina so afraid of Cassie becoming the slayer? Not all slayers were killed. From what I knew, Cassie's grandfather had lived to be almost a hundred years old. She couldn't change what Cassie was. I didn't want anything bad to happen Cassie either. That's why her being s slayer again would help keep her safe. If she carried on the way she was, something would get the best of her eventually.

"Who are your parents?" Tyrone demanded.

Before Cassie had a chance to answer, the double doors burst open. A short dark-haired woman came in. Her long hair fell past her shoulders, black coal lined her eyes and she wore a long black lacy dress. An aura of power shone around her, almost visible under the glare of the glittering chandeliers overhead.

Wonderful, the McGregor witch was here. I hadn't expected her of all people to show up.

"Mother, what are —" Nina gasped then closed her mouth again.

No doubt the council leaders would want to know why the McGregor witch had decided to grace them with her presence. Magda McGregor was infamous in the supernatural world. Not only was she a witch with fae blood but she had been married to an elf slayer. The McGregor family was renowned for their mixed blood and powerful magic.

"Why's my granddaughter been dragged here for interrogation?" Magda put her hands on her hips. "I should have been told about this. You have no right to question her."

"All due respect, Lady McGregor, your granddaughter's been involved in using careless magic. She is attracting creatures from the Nether Realm and we want to know why." Tyrone didn't wither under Magda's glare. "Now, one of you had better tell us who her parents is or do we need to have a blood test performed on her?"

Cassie hesitated. "My mother was Estelle McGregor. And my father's sitting right over there." She inclined her head towards Cal.

All colour drained from the faces of each council leader.

"You're the daughter of the slayer," Katya gasped.

Tyrone's mouth fell open. "Impossible. How can she be your daughter?" he demanded of Cal. "It's forbidden for a slayer and magus to be involved with each other."

Magda's eyes widened but she didn't say anything about Cassie's sudden revelation.

Nina gritted her teeth. "Cassie's lineage isn't important. She is my niece and my adopted daughter and she's fae, not elven. She will never become the slayer. There is no slayer anymore. The slayer died the day my sister was killed. The day you murdering bastards killed her." She gripped Cassie's arm. "Come on, Cassie, we're leaving."

"Sit down, Miss McGregor, you're not going anywhere." Tyrone glared at her.

"Impossible. The elves couldn't have killed your sister. The slayer was killed by monsters that came from the Nether Realm," Katya insisted.

"That might be the official story but I know damn well that's not what happened." Nina glowered at Cal. "He let her die. A magus is supposed to help a slayer, to watch over them. He did none of that. That's why I sure as hell won't allow you to drag Cassie back into this mess. I already lost my sister and Olivia; I won't lose her as well."

They continued to ask more questions about Cassie's upbringing and education. She'd been to Everlight Academy and got her PI licence eighteen. She also did some dancing and modelling (to) when she was younger. Didn't seem to stick to anything, though.

"Cassie's lineage isn't important. What's done is done," Magda insisted. "Nor can you force her to be anything." She took Nina's arm and led her back over to the other side of the room where they could sit down.

"Where did you get that dragon?" Mordora motioned to Murphy, as if noticing him for the first time. "Dragons are rare and they're not pets."

Cassie shrugged. "I found him in some caves whilst hiking through the Ever Realm. Can't give you an exact location since I wasn't following the map."

We both knew that wasn't true. But I could understand why she didn't want to tell the elves that. If they know the truth about Murphy, they would have more power over her.

She didn't reveal anything else about Murphy despite more questioning.

"We should perform a test and see of her powers are indeed a threat," Tyrone said and rose from his seat. He placed the crystal in front of Cassie. "Place your hands on it and I suggest you remove the dragon so its magic doesn't interfere." He reached for Murphy and the dragon snapped at his fingers.

"Murphy, it's okay. Go and sit with Mum."

Murphy growled at Tyrone and blew out a plume of smoke. Reluctantly he glided across the room. Instead of going to Nina, he came over to me.

Hey, little one. I patted his head. *Don't worry, we won't let anything happen to Cassie.*

The doors burst open again as a blonde woman with large gossamer wings came in. Her long blond hair fell down her back. I recognised the fae Queen Silvana Goodwin.

"Sorry I'm late." Two burly guards followed in behind her. "What have I missed?" Silvy demanded. "Why wasn't I informed earlier about one of my subjects being dragged here?"

All four council leaders shot to their feet. Cal and Nina did too so I followed suit.

"Queens Silvana, to what you what do we are the pleasure?" Tyrone bowed his head and approached her.

"I heard you dragged Cassie Morgan in for questioning. I should've been informed about this."

"All due respect, your majesty. Cassandra Morgan isn't fae." Katya crossed her arms. "Nor are you and Lady McGregor needed here."

The queen's eyes flicked over towards Nina and Magda. "She is legally the daughter of Nina Morgan, who is fae. This meeting is over, you have no authority over Cassie. This is absurd."

"Your Majesty, Cassandra is not —" Katya said

"If we test her abilities —" Tyrone spoke up.

"Who are you to question me, elf?" The queen hissed. "You forget who I am. Like it or not she's not subject to your rules, are we clear?"

"For crying out loud." Cassie touched the crystal. "There, I touched it."

Nina rushed over and yanked her hand away. "Enough. We're leaving. Now."

"Wait, we have more questions," Katya protested.

"Your questions are done." The queen raised her chin. "We're all leaving. Last time I checked you have no authority over me."

"She still summoned the baneling. She must be held accountable," Mordora insisted.

"It won't happen again. I assure you." Nina

put a protective arm around Cassie. "My daughter isn't the slayer and never will be."

They left the room with the fae queen.

"We can't just let them leave," I whispered to Cal.

"Come with me."

Cal and I rushed after them. "Wait," Cal called out. "I do have a suggestion. I'd like to offer Cassie a place at the academy and a chance to train as an enforcer."

"Elfhame Academy?" Cassie scoffed. "But I'm not —"

"Absolutely not," Nina snapped. "I've lost one daughter because of your precious academy and the mess she got caught up in here. I'm not about to lose another."

"Agreed. If Cassie wants to go to college, there are other places," Magda said.

"Why would you want me to join the elven enforcers?" Cassie frowned at her father. "Did the council put you up to it?"

Cal shook his head. "The council know nothing of this. Your talents are going to waste in the human realm. You could be incredible with the right training."

"Says the man who let the last slayer die." Nina scoffed.

"I'll think about it," Cassie said finally. "But for now we're done here."

CHAPTER 6

CASSIE

My mind reeled from the entire meeting. I couldn't believe my grandma and Silvy had turned up. Or how everyone kept arguing over my parentage and what I was and wasn't supposed to be. It'd taken everything in me not to scream. I hated people fighting over my life like this. Didn't I have a say in any of this?

After Silvy spoke to my mum and grandma and told them to avoid antagonising the elves any more, she left.

"What's going on?" I demanded of Mum when we reappeared in our living room. "Why do you keep going on about my birth mum's murder? You said it was an open and shut case."

I thought I was done asking questions

about what happened to my birth mum. I had looked at some of the case files myself and it had been an open and shut case. She had been attacked by creatures from the Nether Realm, fought them and lost her life to them. So why was my mum so angry at the elves?

"It was a long time ago, Cassie. The case is closed. From now on I don't want you to have anything to do with the elves or the Nether Realm. I don't want you dragged back into their world."

"Thank goodness that's over with," Grandma remarked and slumped onto the sofa. "Nina, you should have called me sooner. I could have helped you with the Olivia situation as well."

Mum blew out a breath. "I didn't even want you there, Mother. You couldn't help with anything. How did you even know about the meeting?"

I slumped down onto the settee. "I texted her and told her I was being summoned. I thought her presence there might help."

Mum and Grandma had never got along very well. Even before my birth mum had been killed. When Estelle had died, Mum had pretty much cut off all contact with Grandma. Shame, Grandma and I had been close once, but we still spoke to each other every so often.

"Why would you call her?" Mum demanded and motioned towards Grandma. "She's not part of our lives anymore."

"Because she has a lot of experience with the elves. Just because you cut her off doesn't mean I have to."

Grandma raised her chin. "I have the right to see my granddaughter. Olivia already got herself caught up in all of this mess. Clearly I needed to step in."

"What is the big deal?" I glared at Mum. "What are you hiding from me about Liv and my birth mum?"

Mum pinched the bridge of her nose. "There's nothing to tell. Estelle is dead and Liv is gone. Mother, leave us." She inclined her head towards the door. "We've got nothing to discuss with you."

Grandma crossed her arms. "I'm not going anywhere."

Mum turned away from her. "You shouldn't have told the council about Cal being your father either," Mum said. "Elf and fae unions are still frowned on even now. Never mind the fact Estelle was a slayer."

"But *I'm* a slayer. Am I supposed to just hide that fact now? Nothing you say or do is going to change that."

"You can't change what she is," Grandma pointed out. "Estelle wouldn't want her walking away from her heritage."

"Estelle isn't here and she wasn't much of a mother since I was the one always looking after her children," Mum snapped, then turned back to me. "I won't let you get dragged back into that life. It leads to nothing but death." Her hands clenched into fists.

"But my mum ⌒ still trained me to be a slayer and I still have slayer powers. Maybe I should —"

"No. Absolutely not!"

"Like it not, the elves know about Cassie now. The best thing to do is to work with them. For now at least. You don't have to side with them, dear," Grandma told me. "If they want to offer you a place in the academy, let them."

"Mother, we've already lost Estelle and Olivia; do you just expect me to stand back and watch her die too?" Mum glowered at Grandma.

"Do you have a better idea?" Grandma demanded and returned Mum's glare. "We can't just ignore this. Not after everything that happened with Olivia."

"What happened to my mum? If you're hiding something from me, I deserve to know." I put my hands on my hips.

Mum shuddered. "She was killed. There are no words to describe what they did to her."

"You said monsters came through from the Nether Realm and killed her."

Mum nodded. "That's true — that's why the case is closed."

If that were true, why had Mum got so riled up about it? Why had she accused the elves of killing Estelle?

Mum rose and paced up and down. "This is pointless. Cassie, you need to stop looking for things that aren't there. Looking for Olivia is just a waste of time."

I gaped at her. "How can you say that? You can't believe the lies the elves are saying about her being dead? Because is not true!"

"Olivia messed with things she shouldn't have dealt with. She's not coming back and you need to accept that," Mum snapped.

Grandma got up and stepped in between us. "Let's all try to calm down. Cassie, it's up to you if you decide if you want to go to the academy. But I don't think you can ignore this. Your powers are growing and you have a dragon. If the elves view you as a threat —"

"Then I'll deal with it." I stormed off before they either of them could say anything else.

I couldn't handle any more today so I rushed up to my room and locked the door. Slumping onto my bed, I laid down for a while. I didn't know how to feel about Mum's revelation. How could she just give up on Liv? And what really happened to my birth mum? With the way people going on I wondered if there was more to it than I had been told.

Grabbing my laptop, I went into Mum's case files where she kept her PI cases and case files and when she used to be an enforcer. She thought I didn't know how to get to them but I had been looking through her files for years and she had yet to keep me out.

I did a few quick searches but I couldn't find anything on Estelle. I knew my mum and she would definitely keep case files on the death of her sister.

Maybe she just didn't keep them in digital format. I would have a look around for them later. But for now I couldn't stand being in the house any longer. So I climbed out my window along with Murphy and jumped down into the garden. Milan I made my way into town. A few humans sent curious glances my wife will stop nothing unusual there. I stood out with my dark purple hair and pointed ears. Elvin ears. I don't like to admit here but I knew I had elf blood. Elves weren't nice

71

people. What did that make me?

Grabbing some Chinese takeaway food, I headed to Castle Park to eat it on a bench. The park had always been one of my few favourite places to visit. With its gorgeous flower beds and rolling green grass.

I didn't know what to do. Home didn't seem like a good option. I couldn't face Mum again yet. Not after she had completely given up on Liv.

Aside from my sister and my ex-boyfriend, Mike, I didn't have many friends who lived close by. Mike had gone off to the academy when we broke up a few months ago.

After travelling around Elfhame, I'd planned to work with Mum for a while then decide on a uni for next year. Everlight Academy had never felt right for me. Even the fae viewed me as different. I had made a few friends there but they moved on with their lives now.

Now I felt stuck.

I ate my chicken and rice. After a while, I yanked my laptop out of my pack and did a search for my birth mother again and Liv. No records appeared. I didn't know what to make of that. Since Estelle had been the slayer there had to be records of her somewhere. And was

Mum so keen to keep her files on her hidden?

Even though I had been twelve years old when she passed I couldn't remember that much about her. What had happened to her? Had someone covered up her death? And why had Mum given up on Liv?

Murphy had his own foil dish of rice and happily chewed away on its contents.

Was it a coincidence I'd found a dragon or fate?

I did a search for slayers but nothing much appeared. That didn't surprise me. My family weren't big on sharing their secrets with anyone.

Murphy wolfed down the rest of his food, then jumped onto my shoulder and rested his head against mine.

"Thanks, boy."

A motorbike shot through the park and headed straight towards me. Weird, the bike didn't make any noise.

Great. Ash. I'd recognise him anywhere.

Why had he followed me again?

"This is called stalking, you know." I glared at him. "I don't want to talk to you. I've had enough drama for one day, thanks."

"Are you always this prickly? When we were kids you were always happy to see me."

"Me? Prickly?" I snorted. "That's probably

true, but a lot has changed since we were kids. Besides, we're not friends anymore."

Ash climbed off his bike. "I'm happy to see you again too."

"Look, I'm not in the mood for chit chat. Today has been really shit."

Ash sat on the bench next to me and held out an envelope with a wax seal on it. "Maybe this will make you feel better. Or not, judging how much you seem to hate elves now."

"I don't hate all elves. But I sure as hell don't trust them. They've treated me and my family like crap over the years." I grabbed the envelope and tore it open. "Cassandra Morgan, we are pleased to offer you a place at Elfhame Academy." I frowned. "What are you playing at?"

"Not only elves go there. Witches, fae and other supernaturals do as well. Your sister went there and your cousin is enrolled there, too. You had a hard time fitting in at Everlight Academy, didn't you?"

I narrowed my eyes. "How do you know so much?"

"You know I can't reveal my sources." Ash picked Murphy up and leaned back on the bench.

Why didn't Murphy seem bothered by him? Just because Ash had once been my friend didn't make him an ally now. A lot had changed over the years. Yet Murphy acted like Ash was his new best mate.

"Well, if you didn't talk to my mum or sister you must have talked to someone else who knows me." I tapped my chin. "You spoke to Mike, didn't you?" I rolled my eyes. "I should have known. He transferred to the academy a few months ago." Even though we had broken up I still kept tabs on Mike. Just to see what he was up to.

"There's more than an invitation to the academy." Ash gave Murphy some treats from his pocket. "Cal wants you to start training again. Like you did when we were kids."

"Hey, what are you feeding him?"

"Raw meat. I picked some up on the way over. Dragons need meat to become stronger, especially when they're growing."

"I don't believe you." I shook my head.

"About dragons?" He arched one perfect eyebrow.

"No, about joining the enforcers. Why would I do that? Your council wants to lock me up. I'd be walking right into a trap."

"No one is going to lock you up. And you can't keep ignoring your slayer powers."

"And what if I don't want to do that? Everyone keeps telling me what I should and shouldn't do. No one's asking me how I feel about all this."

"Come on, Cass. We both know you miss being a slayer — or at least part of you does. I could see it in your eyes when we fought together back in Elfhame."

"Ash, don't pretend you know me anymore. And definitely don't pretend you're my friend because you're not. I can't trust you and I won't."

"You need a magus, who's better for that job than me? Think about it, what is left for you here?" He motioned around us. "You want to find your sister, don't you?"

"That's really low, using my sister to try and get me to do what you want. You're so much like him now." I crossed my arms.

"You mean Cal? He's not a bad man, Cass. You don't find being the PI fulfilling as you thought it would be, do you?"

"What did you do? Get Mike drunk?"

"No, I spoke to Mike a few weeks ago. But I know a lost soul when I see one. The PI business is Nina's gig. You're still trying to figure out your place in the world." Ash stroked Murphy. "If joining us gets you what you want, why not accept it?"

I grabbed Murphy so fast he yelped in alarm. "You're playing on my emotions because you need something from me. I'm not stupid. You need a slayer to get rid of all the things that are coming out the Nether Realm."

"Good, then you're smart enough to know the council won't stop looking into you. Being with the enforcers would grant you some protection."

"I'm overprotected enough already." I shoved the letter into my jacket. "Do me a favour and don't follow me again."

"That wasn't a no." Ash grinned.

"It wasn't a yes either."

CHAPTER 7

CASSIE

The next few days passed in a blur; I didn't talk to Mum much. She had been livid when I told her I wanted to go to the academy. She said I was mad to go, but what did I have to lose? It was better than being stuck at home. Especially now Mum had given up on Liv. Somehow I knew Mum hadn't told me everything. Not about my birth mum's death either.

Mum won't tell me any more about Liv's case. She said she blamed the elves for Estelle's death because if it were for them Estelle would still be alive. I didn't see the logic in that.

Mum insisted on driving me there the day I was meant to go to the academy. "It's not too late to back out," Mum remarked as we drove up to the bridge that served as an inter-realm crossing.

"Wow, that's the most you said to me in days." I rested my chin on my fist.

Outside, a couple of cars queued behind us. The bridge looked like it disappeared into heavy fog. Four guards were stationed there. Two elves, a fae male and a female. The bridge remained hidden to the humans.

"Liv disappeared after she worked on the academy's island. I don't want anything to happen to you too." Mum tapped the steering wheel, impatient of the guard to come over and check our papers.

"Maybe I can get information about Liv that you couldn't." I bent to make sure Murphy was asleep inside my bag. No way could I risk Murphy being seen by any of the guards. I didn't know how I'd explain having him. Since I hadn't brought him back over the crossing when I left Elfhame the last time I'd been there.

"There's nothing else to find." Mum glanced out the window and huffed out a breath. "What's taking so long?"

"I know there's stuff about Liv's case you haven't told me. Why not?" I demanded. "I'm not a kid anymore. But I guess that's becoming your habit. Not telling me anything."

We both knew there was more about Liv's case she hadn't told me. More than Lucy being possessed and an elf being murdered. Nothing was ever that simple.

"Because it won't change anything. Liv's gone; we both have to learn to live with that." Mum opened her window as an elf and fae guard came over. She plastered on her best business smile and held up her ID.

The other guard came around to my side. I opened my window and handed the elf my licence and college acceptance letter.

The elf's dark eyes widened. "You're elven then?"

Why was that even his business? But that was the elves. Lineage was everything to them.

"Yep. Can we go through now?" I gave a smile that showed too much teeth. "I can't wait to get there."

"It's a brilliant school. Much better than the ones the fae run." The guard waved us through. "Go through and have fun at the academy."

Mum and I closed our windows and headed straight into the mist. Light pulsed around us and for a moment the car floated in nothingness. Then the car shuddered. Murphy yelped and shot out of my bag onto my lap. The light grew brighter until the mist rolled back and revealed the other end of the bridge. The car juddered as it fully emerged from the mist. The sky appeared a brighter blue, the trees green. Everything looked much brighter than the grey monotony of the human realm.

Murphy jumped onto the dashboard and huffed in excitement. I wondered if he was happy to be back in his realm. Being stuck in the human realm must have taken its toll on him.

We drove over the bridge and onto the dirt road. The elves weren't big on paved roads outside of their cities so the car bounced around quite a lot.

I didn't bother talking to Mum anymore. What would I even say? She didn't support me going here and all the answers she'd given me so far had been vague.

I still didn't know what to expect when I got to the academy. What if people found out about me being a slayer? I remember the way people used to look at my birth mum whenever she took me anywhere. The glares, the whispers and suspicious looks. Being a slayer didn't make you friends. It gave you a lot of enemies.

Mum pulled over. "Are you sure you want

to do this? If the other elves find out what you are, you'll have nothing but problems." She slammed her hands on the steering wheel. "You don't have to go there just to get information on Liv. There's nothing to find."

"I'm not. I want to know more about being a slayer again. We both know this is the only place that can teach me about that."

"That's not true. You could train with the fey guardians or even the trackers. I thought after you got your license you would want to work with me. If you want to go to college, you could go anywhere in the world."

"Guardians and trackers aren't slayers. Can we please just get there?" I sighed. "I'm a big girl. I can fight my own battles. Besides, having a break from each other will do us both good."

Mum flinched. "I'm trying to protect you."

"Not telling me everything about Liv's case doesn't protect me." I glared at her. "Don't I deserve to know?"

Mum hesitated. "Liv wasn't perfect, you know that."

"What's that supposed to mean?" I furrowed my brow.

"Liv was sleeping with Jared."

"But Liv already had a girlfriend." I gaped at her when realisation hit me. "You don't think Liv killed him and used Lucy as a sacrifice, do you? Because that's bloody ridiculous!"

Mum shook ahead. "Of course not. But Jared was into some pretty dark magics, not just necromancy."

"Okay, what else do you know?"

"I think someone killed Liv because of Jared."

My eyes widened. "And you didn't tell me this, why?"

"Because I can't prove any of it. The elves shut down my case. I barely got anything when I came here." Mum leaned back in her seat. "No one would talk to me. The elves blocked me at every turn. Now you want to join them."

"I'll find out what happened to Liv. Think about it. This is my one chance to get close to them. You might have some elven blood but you don't look like them the way I do."

"I don't want to lose you. You know what the elves are like, they'll never accept you. Especially not when they figure out who and what you are." Mum took hold of my hand. "I think something came out of the Nether Realm and killed Liv. That's why I don't want you to be a slayer."

"You won't lose me. I can handle myself

and I have Murphy."

Mum snorted. "I doubt that tiny dragon will offer much protection."

Murphy puffed out his chest and I smiled.

I gasped when the island came into view. I'd known Elfhame Academy took up an entire island but I hadn't expected it to look so big.

As we drew closer to the island, a massive bridge lowered down and more armed guards came over to us. All elves this time.

Mum showed them her ID and I showed them my letter. The guard scrutinised it before they finally waved us through. Mum drove across the bridge and I took everything in. Trees spread out in a thick green blanket and tall towers of stone dotted the horizon.

"Never expected this place to be so big."

Mum grimaced. "It has to be. Lots of supernaturals come here. And of course the Elhanan has a base and a training programme here."

The sweeping road wound around the thick canopy of forest. A lot of the island looked to be covered in thick trees.

Soon, the castle came into view. All imposing grey stone turrets and towers. I half expected archers to bear down on us.

People were everywhere as we drew closer.

Most of them elves. Tall, ethereal with dark hair or blond hair but there were wolves and other animal shifters. Didn't see many of them round Colchester. Most of them lived in a small island near Cornwall.

A knot of dread formed in my stomach. I'd never fit in anywhere. What if these people treated me like an outcast too?

That wouldn't be unusual. I'd been an outcast as long as I could remember. The fae had never accepted me and I doubted the elves would be any different.

Mum finally found a place to park, then unloaded my bags from the boot.

"You don't have to come with me. I have a map." I slung my bag over my shoulder and grabbed the handle of my suitcase.

The moment Murphy got out of the car he dove headlong into the trees. He must have been excited to be surrounded by so much nature again. And to be back in his home realm. My stomach twisted tighter.

Mum teared up. "I know you don't need me with you. You never even liked me walking you to school." She flung her arms around me. "I'm gonna miss you so much."

I returned her hug. Despite our differences, she was still my mum. The only real mother I'd ever known. Nothing would ever change that. "I'll miss you, too."

"Be careful and keep your guard up." Mum fumbled in her pocket and held out a silver bracelet. "I got you a transpo bracelet. So you can teleport home if you need to."

"They cost a fortune. How did you —?"

Mum shrugged. "I know people. There's a couple of backup crystals too in case you damage it." Mum slipped it on my wrist. "Promise you'll call regularly, and if you get into any trouble —"

"I'll call," I promised and hugged her one last time.

Mum stayed by the car as I made my way towards the castle.

No sign of Murphy, though. I felt a little lost without him being close by. The knot in my stomach grew tighter.

I took a deep breath. *It's now or never. I can do this.*

CHAPTER 8

CASSIE

As I made my way towards the castle, I glanced round for Murphy. Where had he flown off to? What if he didn't come back? Guess I had got used to him being around me all the time.

My heart pounded in my ears. We'd never really been apart since I'd found him a couple of months ago and it felt weird not having him hanging around.

The sweeping stone towers loomed over me, the diamond paned window staring down at me like watchful, disapproving eyes. Almost like the academy itself could tell what I was. I shook off the feeling, knowing it was stupid.

Murphy? I called out to him with my mind.

No sign of him appeared.

Murphy, come here!

Goddess, what if I'd lost him? What if he'd run off because he didn't like being cooped up with me?

I pushed my fears away and carried on heading towards the academy's entrance. Being surrounded by so many gorgeous elves made me a little self-conscious. My body had way more curves than elves usually had. My dark purple hair made me stand out. But I'd always loved my hair and wouldn't change it to suit someone's ideal image of beauty. If that left me an outcast so be it.

Murphy! I yelled this time and cast my senses out. His presence seemed to be darting all over the place. *He must be excited, that's all,* I told myself.

As I drew closer to the castle's entrance, I spotted a group of elves crowded around, holding up their phones and throwing things at someone tied to a flagpole. So elves humiliated people too. What a shock.

I moved through the crowd so I could get a better look. My heart lurched. Lucy Grey.

She had long brown hair pulled up in a high ponytail, her blue eyes were wide with fear and blood dripped down her pale face from a gash on her forehead. Her gossamer wings were tied down along with the rest of her.

I'd known Lucy had come here, but I hadn't expected to run into her so soon.

"Hey, what's going on?" I asked a blond-haired elf girl.

The girl had on a Gucci pink dress and matching heels. Her lip curled when she took in my jeans and hoodie. "We're making a murderer pay for their crimes. Don't tell me you haven't heard of how she killed one of us?"

"Oh, I've heard." *More than you know.* Still couldn't understand why they wanted to take revenge for Jared of all people. He had been a lowlife necromancer by their standards.

I'd blamed Lucy for Liv's disappearance at first too, before I'd gotten to know her. She had been a victim as much as anyone. But that didn't make her responsible for what happened to Jared. Just because he was connected to a noble family.

They continued to throw rocks at her.

An elven male pulled out a knife. "Let's cut off those pretty wings of hers."

"Cut her ears too," the blonde girl called out. "Make them pointed then cut them off."

"Slit her throat!" someone else yelled.

I scanned the crowd for signs of anyone in authority who might put an end to this. There didn't seem to be any teachers around. Or if there were they blended in with everyone else.

Why hadn't Ash or Cal come out? I'd expected them to be here to pester me with more questions.

Why wasn't anyone stepping forward to stop this? Lucy had been cleared of all charges. But I couldn't say this surprised me. People were always quick to blame others. It didn't matter what race you were.

I couldn't let them hurt Lucy. We might not be friends but she didn't deserve this. Not after everything that happened to her.

I left my case and bag near the steps and triggered my anti-theft charms so no one would steal them.

Still no Murphy either. Typical.

Pushing my way through the crowd, I stepped up to the ringleader that I decided to call Smiley. "Hey, back off and leave her alone."

The elf's eyes widened. "Stay out of this." He leaned closer to me and sniffed. "You stink of fae."

I smirked. "Oh, I'm so much more than that."

Smiley snorted. "And what are you gonna do about it?"

"Kick your skinny arse for one thing. She never killed anyone, so back the hell off."

"How would you know that?" another elven male demanded.

Great, I just had to open my big mouth. "Let's just say I have more knowledge of the case then you do. Now —"

Someone came up behind me and caught me a headlock.

Really? They wanted to try this?

I stamped on his foot and elbowed him in the gut, caught hold of his arm and tossed him to the ground. Another one came at me. I punched him so hard he crashed into the wall next to us. Slayer strength came in handy sometimes.

Another elf came at me. He threw a punch. I dodged, spun and knocked his legs out from under him. Smiley threw a bolt of light at me.

I dodged it, then raised my hand. Purple light flared between my fingers and more power rose inside me. How the heck could I get these morons to back off?

An image of Liv's smiling face flashed through my mind and my anger grew. Light shot from my hand, blowing up a large statue behind us.

Smiley and his cronies finally backed away.

I grabbed his knife and threw it at his head. It embedded itself an inch above him in the wall. "Next time I won't miss." I hurried over to Lucy and burned off the ropes with my magic.

"Cassie, what the fuck are you doing here?" Lucy hissed.

"You're welcome." I yanked the ropes off around her legs. "Are you alright? Do you need a healer?"

Someone ran over to us as the crowd finally dispersed. A few elves moved out of our way. Good, I'd made friends real quick here. Not. Well, nothing unusual there. I couldn't just stand back and let them torture Lucy anyway.

"Cassie, what are you doing here?" Mike asked. He looked just as I remembered. Same floppy brown hair, green eyes and dimples. He wore his usual jeans and rumpled shirt.

"Mike!" I threw my arms around him. "Goddess, it's so good to see you."

Mike returned my hug. "Hey, Cass. I've missed you."

"Me too. I mean, I missed you." I shook my head. Goddess, could I sound any more stupid?

"What are you doing here?" Lucy growled at me. "Have you come to interrogate me again? This is ridiculous. Are you ever gonna stop following me around?"

I rolled my eyes. "Not everything is about you." I flashed my letter in front of her. "I go here now, too. And I was just trying to help."

Lucy's mouth fell open as she grabbed my letter and read through it. "What? How? No way! Stay the hell away from me!" She tossed my letter aside and stormed off without saying another word.

Mike raised his brows. "I see you're making friends already."

"I couldn't let them hurt her. She didn't kill anyone." I glanced over at the statue. "Crap. Trust me to get into trouble before I get inside the building."

"I can fix this." Mike went over and chanted something. Light flashed and the statue reformed.

"Nice." I grinned. "You always were good with magic tricks."

"And you always were quick to throw punches." Mike shook his head. "But you admit, I'm surprised to see you here. I didn't think this place was your scene."

"I have my reasons for coming here. Do you think I should have let them torture her, then?" I put my hands on my hips.

"No, but you need to be careful. Don't make enemies here. The elves aren't to be messed with. A lot of the students who go here are from highborn noble families who have a lot of power and influence in this realm."

I headed back to grab my case and bag. Looked like someone had thrown a fireball at them as I noticed the edges were now a little blackened. But at least the stuff inside wouldn't have been damaged. I kept protection charms on everything. Didn't have much choice nowadays since Murphy often destroyed things.

"Hey, my charms held up." Mike grinned.

"Yeah, this bag came halfway around Elfhame with me." I swung it over my shoulder. *Murphy!* I called him again.

This had to be the longest we'd been apart. Excluding the time he went out at night when I was usually sleeping. Where had he gone? And why wouldn't he answer my calls? I still felt his presence so he hadn't left the island, but what had he gotten up to?

"Come on, everyone's gathering in the main hall. First years get tested to give them an idea of what classes to take. It's all choice, though." Mike chatted away as we made our way up the steps. "I still can't believe you're here. How've you been? I'm sorry about your sister."

I flinched and never knew how to react to that. Sure, people said the words but they meant nothing. I hesitated, unsure what to even say. No way could I tell him why I'd really come to the academy. He'd just interfere if I told him the truth. Mike'd never really been supportive of me being a PI either. It was one of the reasons why we'd broken up.

"Thanks." I glanced behind us but still couldn't see Murphy.

"Is something wrong?" Mike frowned. "Did you forget something?"

"No. Let's go."

The great hall looked like a theatre with rows of seats from the floor all the way to the ceiling. Different flags for the various noble families hung from the oak walls. The tile floor gleamed. It reminded me of the council's meeting hall. Mike told me where new arrivals were supposed to sit on the bottom rows. To my surprise, Mike came and sat with me.

"I still can't believe you're here." Mike shook his head. "What made you come? I thought you wanted to go travelling for a year."

"A lot has happened in my life since we last saw each other." I glanced around. Still no Murphy. No Ash either. I thought he would have come to greet me at least.

Had the Elhanan changed their minds about me? That wouldn't surprise me if they had. I'd stay until I found out what happened to Liv. It'd taken me this long just to get onto the island. No way would I leave without getting answers.

Lucy sat a few rows down from me. She threw me a glare. Geez, you'd think she'd be grateful I'd got her down. I'd only been trying to help. A plaster now covered her forehead. People moved away from her when they spotted her and everyone refused to sit next to her. My heart went out to her. Someone yelled the word "murderer" and Lucy ducked her head.

I considered going to sit with her but I knew she wouldn't appreciate the gesture. So I remained where I was. But I'd try talking to her later just to make sure she was alright.

"Didn't expect you'd be here." A girl with long dark purple hair, blue eyes and wearing black jeans and a black leather camisole came over and sat beside me. "I guess that explains why Auntie Nina has been on the phone complaining to my mum every day."

I breathed a sigh of relief when I spotted my cousin, Jolie McGregor. "Hi." I gave her a quick hug.

"Let me guess, you've come to investigate Liv's case." She shook her head. "You'd be better leaving that mess alone, Cass."

I gritted my teeth and bit back a retort. Now wasn't the time to argue with her. But I'd expected her to be on my side.

A large dais stood in the centre of the room. Around thirty people sat nearby. Some were elves, some witches and fae. A beautiful elf woman with long blond hair stepped up onto the dais. "Welcome to a new term of at Elfhame Academy, students. I'm Eloise Gardner, the chancellor. I'm excited to see so many new and familiar faces." She smiled and rambled on. "I'm sure you're all looking forward to the start of a new chapter in your lives."

I almost rolled my eyes at that and scanned the room further. There were more non-elves here than I expected. But the majority of people in the room were elves. Their power rolled over me like waves crashing against rock.

Murphy? I called again.

He'd been gone for ages and the longer he stayed gone, the more my nerves grew.

"Now we'll begin the sorting ceremony. Each first-year student will be tested and given a list of potential classes to choose from," the chancellor announced. "This is to make it easier for everyone to choose the right classes for them. But everything is your choice. These are only suggestions, and you don't have to choose them if you don't want to."

A large crystal stood on the podium. Another teacher started calling out names and one by one students went up to it. They'd touch the crystal and it flared with light. Whilst another teacher handed them a piece of paper with classes written on it.

"So what are your plans while you're here?" Mike whispered.

I hesitated. What could I say? "To find my sister and find out what being a slayer means"? No, that wouldn't go over well.

Instead, I said, "I'm looking for a new start. A chance to figure out what I am."

"That's good. Glad you're not…"

"Not what?" I narrowed my eyes.

He shook his head. "Never mind."

I knew what he meant. He meant wallowing in grief. Nope, tears wouldn't help me find Liv. Now I'd find out what really happened to my sister.

Light bounced around the ceiling as something darted around.

Murphy, my senses told me and my heart leapt.

Murphy, get down here!

The light bounced around some more then darted towards me. Orbs sparkled as Murphy materialised in my lap.

"Where've you been?" I hissed.

Murphy purred and huffed. I gathered him up in my bag and told him to stay there.

"Is that a dragon?" Mike whispered.

"Wow, you're well behind if you don't know about the dragon," Jolie remarked to him.

Murphy relayed images of the woods to me and feelings of happiness washed over me.

I stared at him in shock. He'd never done that before. He could sometimes say the odd word or two in thought but nothing like that. Had our bond grown stronger?

"Yeah, he's mine. Long story." My senses tingled as I felt someone's eyes on me.

Ash stood lurking on the other side of the hall. Cal sat nearby.

"How did you get a dragon?" Mike whispered. "Dragons aren't supposed to exist anymore. I doubt you're allowed to bring one to the academy."

"I'll tell you later." If the academy had a problem with Murphy, they'd just have to deal with it. No way would I make him leave.

"Cassandra Morgan," the teacher called out my name.

My heart dropped to my stomach. "Hold him." I gave the bag with Murphy in it to Mike.

Murphy growled at Mike, leapt from the bag and climbed onto my shoulder.

"Stay with Mike," I hissed at him.

Murphy snorted and wrapped himself around my neck.

Murphy, go and stay with Mike! I glared at him.

"Murphy, come here." Jolie motioned towards herself but my dragon ignored her.

Maybe he just didn't like Mike given how they'd only just met. But I'd never seen him dislike anyone before. All eyes fell on me. The girl with the dragon.

I sighed and stood up, making my way towards the dais.

"Um, Miss Morgan, you can't do the test with a... An animal attached to you." The teacher shifted from foot to foot and took a step back as Murphy and I approached.

Whispers rang through the crowd. Guess I should have expected that. Most supernaturals thought dragons to be extinct. Or just a myth. Yet here I had one riding around on my shoulder.

Murphy, go, I demanded. *Go and wait outside.*

He still didn't budge.

What was with the sudden separation anxiety? He'd been gone for ages earlier.

I couldn't force him off me in front of all these people. My mind raced as I struggled with what to do.

Murphy, go to Ash.

To my amazement, he took off and flew straight to Ash. Murphy plonked himself on Ash's shoulder. Ash's eyes widened but he said nothing.

I placed my hands on the crystal. It flared with a rainbow of different colours. Energy vibrated between my fingers. A collective grasp ran through the crowd. The orb had turned different colours for the other students but not like this. The orb hummed and pulsed with energy.

"You can let go now, Miss Morgan," the teacher said with alarm in his voice.

But I couldn't. Orbs of light danced in front of my eyes. It tugged at my powers. My hair whipped around my face as I stood mesmerised. The light expanded and slowly formed into a swirling portal. Lightning flashed between my fingers.

Murphy shot towards me and landed on my shoulder. I pulled back, still dazed. The portal fizzled out and faded.

Holy crap, what had I done? Why had I done that? My power didn't work like that.

The chancellor came over. "What are you?" she asked with narrowed eyes. "No one can open portals like that."

Cal shock to his feet and rushed over. "She's a new recruit for the enforcers. Cassie, why don't you sit down? Chancellor, please continue the sorting ceremony. I'm sure you have a lot more students to get through."

The chancellor looked like she wanted to protest but I headed back to my seat. People's gazes followed me. Even Lucy stared.

Well, I'd definitely made a lasting impression. I just hoped it wouldn't lead to more problems.

CHAPTER 9

ASH

That had been a close call. I had felt the crystal bringing Cassie's powers to the surface. Cal had mentioned we'd have to watch her in case anything happened. Neither of us had expected the crystal to do that. I wanted to rush down there to help her but Cal had beaten me to it.

I'd been surprised when Murphy had come over to me. I didn't mind. He was a cute little thing.

I headed over to Cassie once the sorting ceremony was over. Murphy stayed perched on my shoulder.

I eyed Mike Loken, a witch from what I've heard. Cassie's ex-boyfriend. I hoped he wouldn't get in the way of her training. Having a slayer running around proved dangerous already. Had she forgotten everything her mum had taught her about keeping her true nature of secret? From what I'd heard she had fought off several elves who had been hounding Lucy Grey.

Mike's jaw tightened when he saw me. "Cass, do you know Ash?"

"Something like that." Cassie scowled at me.

Mike's eyes widened. "But he's Elhanan and you're—"

"We should get going." I gave Mike a hard look. "We're working together." Something about him rubbed me the wrong way.

"Right." Cassie grabbed Murphy off my shoulder. "Let's go."

"Wait, what's going on?" Mike furrowed his brow. "Why would you be working with him? You're not an enforcer."

"Come on." I motioned for Cassie to follow. By the nether, I hoped Mike wasn't going to cause us any trouble.

"Not now, Mike." Cassie shook her head.

Mike looked like he was about to follow but I gave him a warning look.

"Your boyfriend isn't going to be a problem, is he?"

Her eyes widened. "He's *not* my boyfriend. And what's it to you?"

"Good. You need to focus on your slayer duties. Not have distractions."

"I'll be sure to remember that." Cassie snorted.

"Here are a list of classes you can choose from. Along with a training schedule." Cal handed her a couple of pieces of paper.

Cassie frowned. "I have a schedule?"

Cal lowered his voice, "As a slayer, you have certain duties as a slayer and we need to get your powers under control. You must keep this a secret. Don't go running around telling people what you are."

"That won't be a problem."

I hoped Mike wouldn't be a problem. There was something about him I never liked but I couldn't be sure why.

Cassie pulled out her map. "Where will I be living?"

"The housing blocks aren't far from here. Your bags've already been sent there. I want to show something first."

We left Cal and headed out. I started showing Cassie around. We headed up to the castle that served as the main part of the academy. Along with the Practical Magic, Dark Arts and other towers. After showing her where those were, we moved on. There were bikes and boards that allowed people to travel around the island on. It was too far to walk everywhere. There were spell circles too, but it was safer if she didn't use those.

Afterward, we headed to the Elhanan Tower. It loomed over us all imposing grey stone and opaque windows.

"This is where the enforcers work?" Cassie arched an eyebrow.

"Yeah, what were you expecting?"

"I don't know. Maybe an underground bunker given how shady you are."

"We're not shady. We keep the peace in Elfhame and we are the first line of defence for the elves."

The tower loomed stark against the indigo sky. It might not look like much on the outside but inside it was impressive.

We headed through the main entrance and two guards stood on duty. Both tall muscular elves. I showed them my badge and a beam of light shot down from the ceiling, scanning me.

Cassie showed them her ID and the scanner shot over her, then lingered over Murphy.

"What's that?" Cassie took a step back.

"It's a scanner. It has your energy signature on file now and Murphy's. So you can come and go from the building."

"Do I get a badge too?" Cassie looked

hopeful.

"No. Only fully trained agents get them. Plus, you're not here to become an enforcer."

"I'm not?" She frowned.

"That's because I've been an enforcer for a while now. I joined when I was sixteen and spent the last three years studying at the academy. I graduated last year."

Once we got through the security I went over the training schedule with her.

"You'll be training with me in. Both in magic and weapons," I explained.

Cassie glanced at the schedule. "How am I gonna have time for classes?"

"That's why you have a schedule. Besides, you only have classes three days a week. That gives you plenty of time training."

"Yeah, everything is mapped out. Why do we need to do training at weekends?"

"Because you haven't trained as a slayer in over seven years. And you need to get your powers under control."

Her lip curled. "Wow, you have changed a lot. You were much more fun when we were kids."

"Cass, we're not kids anymore. We don't have time for fun. Any more questions?"

"Yeah, why did the portal open when I touched that crystal?"

"The crystal draws magic to the surface and reacts to it. Your slayer and magus powers must have reacted. Hence the need for training. Plus there is no guarantee you will be able to open portals since that's a magus' job, not a slayer."

"Okay, when can we start on my sister's case?"

I should have known this was coming. I couldn't blame her. If I had any family who disappeared, I'd want to find them too. I pulled a file out of my jacket. "Here's everything I know about the case. But it's already been closed."

I had looked over everything we had on her sister's case last night and hadn't found anything new. Although I had agreed to help I doubted there would be much left to find.

What did she expect find?

All indications were Olivia Morgan died the night of the explosion. It didn't matter no body had been found. Liv had been close to where the explosion originated.

"You do know she had an affair with Jared, don't you?" I asked.

She nodded. "I know. Still not sure why, though. She never told me anything about him."

"Sometimes we don't know people as well

as we think we do."

Cassie looked away. "They wouldn't let my mum go to Liv's flat here on the island. Can you show me where it is?"

"All of her stuff has been moved out and boxed up."

"I still need to see it."

We teleported to the housing block. A small square tower block of flats. Used by teachers and other people who worked around the island.

I broke through the evidence tape on the door and opened it. Inside stood an empty living room with whitewashed walls and a threadbare carpet. A stack of boxes were near the door, marked with evidence labels. Looked like I'd been wrong about everything being moved out.

"What happened to the furniture?" Cassie glanced around with a frown.

"It probably all got taken out. Most of the flats in this block are rented along with furniture."

Cassie went and opened a box. She pulled a few things out including a shirt and photo.

"Can you give me a few minutes alone?" Cassie didn't look at me.

"Sure. I'll be in the bedroom. I'll check and

see if they left anything." I doubted they would have but I'd give her some time alone. Stepping into the doorway, I glanced back as she sank to the floor.

My heart ached for her. Should I comfort her? I wanted to, but I knew she didn't trust me anymore. She wouldn't welcome the comfort.

Murphy whined and wrapped his tiny body around her.

Odd. Dragons weren't known for being affectionate. Yet Cassie and this dragon had a bond. It made me more curious about her.

I checked round the bedroom and bathroom. Both rooms remained bare and empty. Everything had been packed up.

After a few minutes, I headed back out. Cassie sat staring at a photo of her sister.

"Do you really think she's still alive?" I surprised myself by asking.

"I don't care what everyone says. I know she's out there somewhere. If she were dead, I would know it."

"But the evidence —"

She scrambled to her feet. "Not everything is about evidence, Ash. Sometimes you just know things when it comes to people you love. Haven't you lost someone?"

"I guess not." The only person I'd truly lost

was her and now she'd come back into my life again.

"No one? What about your family?" Cassie arched an eyebrow. "Not even your mum?"

I winced. "I'm surprised you remember that." My mother died when I was very young. I barely even remembered her. It had just been me and my dad growing up.

"Of course I do. We spent practically every day together up until Estelle was killed."

I didn't like talking about my past. "I never had the chance to know her, did I? Come on, do you want help taking the stuff out of here."

"I guess. I'm not leaving all of this here."

"Where are you going to put it all?"

"I'll take it to my room." She heaved two boxes under her arms.

I grabbed a couple more boxes. "Where is your room?"

"The letter said the magic user housing block. Do they really segregate housing between different species?"

I nodded. "It's not as regimented as it used to be. Some fae do live in the elven block now. But most people tend to stick to their own race."

"Some things never change." Cassie rolled her eyes. "You'd think supernaturals would have evolved beyond racism by now."

"You don't like elves," I pointed out.

"I don't dislike all elves. Just the ones in authority."

"Like me you mean."

"I don't know you anymore, Ash."

I could tell she'd distrusted me from our first meeting but it didn't bother me. I wasn't here to make friends. I had a job to do.

Murphy circled around our heads and jumped onto my shoulder.

"He likes you."

"All dragons like me."

She laughed. "Why?"

I shrugged. "They just do."

"Must be your winning personality."

Nope, it's because I'm like them.

We teleported to the housing block. Murphy danced about as we headed inside the foyer.

"I hope he'll be okay when I'm in classes. He doesn't like being on his own for too long," Cassie remarked. "I hate putting him in a cage."

"Dragons don't cope well in cages and you won't be able to have him in some classes. Animals aren't allowed."

Cassie turned to me. "Where else can I put him? He goes almost everywhere with me."

"I'll see if I can sort something out."

As we headed up to her floor in the lift, I dropped off the boxes and headed out.

I knew working with her wouldn't be easy but that girl was trouble.

CHAPTER 10

CASSIE

I fumbled with my key and prayed my room looked liveable. When I went to Everlight Academy, the rooms had always looked immaculate but this was a university. Liv's flat had been pretty sparse so I didn't know what to expect. Or if I'd have a roommate either. Back at Everlight Academy, I'd had a room to myself and wanted the same thing here. Especially with Murphy flying around. He sometimes stole things and that would only lead to more chaos.

I put the boxes down for a moment and glanced at my paperwork. To my dismay, it said my dorm had three bedrooms. That meant I would have two roommates. Crap, couldn't Cal have put me up in my own room given how desperate he'd been for me to come here?

How was I supposed to keep my big secret by having roommates around? I might not have acted like a slayer in years but I remembered what the life was like. I couldn't guarantee my roommates would be safe. Since a slayer could be attacked by things at any moment. I had half a mind to call Ash and demand he move me somewhere else. But I didn't want to demand things on the very day I'd arrived.

What would I tell my roommates? *Oh, sorry I might attract monsters. By the way I live with a dragon?*

The door finally opened and I gasped when I found Lucy inside the narrow hallway with its beige walls and coffee coloured carpet.

She growled at me. "What are you doing here? Are you stalking me now? This is ridiculous!"

Yep, this was a nightmare. Of all the people I could be roommates with, why did it have to be her? I didn't have anything against her, but I knew she didn't think much of me.

"Er... Looks like we are roommates." I held up my info pack.

"There has to be a mistake. I'm not living with you." She crossed her arms and glowered at me.

"I can't say I wanna live with you either."

"Go then. Get out!" Lucy motioned towards the door.

I shook my head. "I don't have anywhere else to go."

"Go to the housing office and ask for another room. You're not staying here."

"Hey, this is my dorm too. It's not like I chose this one." I guessed no one else would have wanted to be her roommate either.

Lucy snorted. "Yeah right. You've come here so you can pester me more about the case again, haven't you?"

"Not everything I do is about my sister's case," I snapped. "Plus, I saved you earlier. The least you can do is let me use my own room."

"You saved me so you could question me more. Not because you wanted to help."

"Okay, fine. The next time they tie you up and stone you I promise I won't interfere." I grabbed two of the boxes. One burst open and spilled its contents onto the floor. I gave a cry of alarm as objects rolled everywhere.

A photo of me and Liv together hit the floor and smashed. A few stray tears dripped down my cheeks. I had struggled not crying seeing the empty flat earlier. Seeing our favourite photo of us together now broken hurt.

Lucy picked it up instead. "I'm — I'm sorry. I didn't mean to make you cry."

I shook my head. "It's not you. I'm just really tired of everyone telling me to forget about this and move on." I pushed my hair off my face.

"Here, I'll help you pick this stuff up." Lucy grabbed a few items and shoved them back into the box.

"Thanks. Who's our other roommate?"

She shook her head. "We don't have another roommate."

"But it says on the welcome pack there's three rooms here. Is the third room empty?"

"There is no third room either. That's my room." She motioned to an open doorway. "That door leads to the bathroom and the only empty room — your room — is on the other side of the hall."

"Why would they say there's three bedrooms here then?"

Lucy shrugged. "Must have got it wrong."

Somehow I doubted that. But I didn't say anything as I headed down the hall. I stopped when energy vibrated against my skin. When I checked again there was nothing there but a bare wall. Weird, I guessed I was imagining things.

After a while, I managed to get everything into my room. I piled the boxes of Liv's stuff up in the corner. The room looked bigger than I expected with bare beige walls. A single bed, wardrobe, chest of drawers, both mismatched and a desk with a chair.

I dropped my case on the bed and grabbed my laptop. I inserted the disk Ash had given me and waited. Letters and numbers flashed over the screen as the programme decrypted itself. Ash had given me classified stuff. Interesting. Whilst it decrypted I packed my stuff away. I couldn't bring myself to go through Liv's stuff here. It didn't feel right somehow.

Murphy flitted around the room so I hung his hammock up with a spell so he'd have something to sleep on.

Going through the files didn't reveal much. Most of it I was stuff I already knew. Somehow I'd expected the elves to have loads of insight. To know loads of secrets but aside from Jared being Liv's boyfriend there was nothing. Weird, she was in a serious relationship with Hannah, another fae, from what I'd last heard. Liv had been devoted to her girlfriend so I didn't understand why she had a fling with Jared. She didn't even go for men very often as she had always preferred women.

They did have some CCTV footage of Liv and Jared sitting in a booth talking. They didn't look cosy or romantic. It made me wonder if Liv had been romantically involved with him. I knew my sister and she wasn't her type at all.

A pang of guilt settled in my chest like a heavy stone. If I had come back sooner, maybe things will be different. If only I'd talked to her. Found out what had been going on in her life. But we had been so focused on getting Mum out of trouble. After Lucy had escaped from custody, the elves threatened to imprison Mum and spellbind Liv. Since we didn't fall under the fae courts the elves had got jurisdiction as Mum was in their territory when Lucy escaped.

Liv had tried to handle things on her own but she had called me for help. I still hated myself for not getting there sooner. Liv had sent a reaper to come and get me whilst I had been travelling around Elfhame.

Reaper.

I hadn't seen Lily since she transported me back from Elfhame. Although I'd called for her a few times. Mum said Lily didn't always seem to show up but could hear people's calls.

"Lily," I called out. "Lily, I need to talk to

you."

Nothing.

She must have heard me as Mum always called her the same way.

"Lily!"

Still nothing.

"Reaper, reaper, I summon you before me." I chanted the old rhyme and hoped it would work.

Nothing.

"Come on, Lily. I know you can hear me." I tapped my foot against the side of the bed. "I just want to talk."

Murphy perched on his hammock and watched me.

"What will it take to bring that reaper here?" I asked him. "Not sure if bringing myself to the point of death is something I fancy doing."

Maybe a different spell would work.

I grabbed a pen and paper and started scribbling out different words. What kind of spell would bring a reaper here? Maybe Lily would just ignore it.

"Reaper, reaper, who inspires fear, get yourself over here." Not the best spell but maybe it'd get her attention. "Come on, Lily."

I opened my case and shoved the clothes into the wardrobe. I found a tin in there and realised Mum must have put in. She always baked things when she got stressed.

"Too bad I don't have anyone to share these biscuits with, huh, Lily?"

Smoke whirled around the room, taking the form of the skull.

My heart leapt. Lily.

The smoke shifted into a woman with long dark pink hair. She wore her usual purple dress and white and purple striped tights.

"Did you say biscuits?" Lily arched an eyebrow. "Chocolate ones?"

"There's chocolate chip cookies and shortbread. Mum bakes when she's stressed out. So there's probably a lot of food here."

"Ooh, goddess, I miss food." Lily inhaled the biscuits. She grabbed one and moaned. "Wow, your mum can bake." She grabbed more and shoved them into her mouth. "So what's with all the summoning spells? I hate those."

"I need to ask you about my sister."

She held up a hand. "Whoa, let me stop you right there, kid. I'm not an errand girl or some PI source."

"No, you're the Grim Reaper and I need to know what happened to my sister." I rose from the bed. "You helped bring me back from Elfhame."

"Yeah, but I was different. I helped your sister."

"So why can't you help me?" I put my hands on my hips. "You've helped my mum out before on cases. You helped bring me back from Elfhame,"

"That's different. I've been friends with Nina for over a decade. Even worked with her when I was a social worker."

"If you can help Liv and my mum, why can't you help me?"

"Because you want to know if she's dead. There are rules about that sort of thing."

"Come on, what would you do if your sister went missing?" I racked my brain for ideas on how to convince her to help. "Or someone else you cared about?" I didn't know Lily well enough to know if she had any loved ones. From what I know she had once been a witch and a social worker before she'd been killed. No idea how she became a reaper, though.

Murphy flew over and grabbed a cookie.

"Yikes! You still have that dragon?" Lily's eyes widened.

"Yeah. He's my best mate."

"Cassie, do you want —" Lucy froze when she came in. "Holy crap. Lily!" She rushed over and hugged her.

I frowned and wondered why anyone would hug a reaper. I'd be scared of dying from their touch.

Lily grinned and returned her hug. "Hey, kid. You doing okay?"

"You know each other?" My brows rose.

"Yeah, Lucy is one of my foster kids." Lily ruffled her hair. "I've known her since she was tiny."

Wow, I knew Lucy had been in foster care, but I'd never imagined she might have worked with Lily.

"I'm okay, I guess." Lucy clung to Lily a while longer. "It's been rough since... You know."

Yeah, I knew full well what she meant. But if I couldn't get Lily to give me an answer maybe Lucy could.

"So are you gonna tell me what you know about my sister or not?" I repeated and gave Lucy a pointed look. She owed me for saving her. The least she could do was make Lily answer my question.

"I can't —" Lily protested.

"Lil, tell Cassie the truth." Lucy pulled away from her. "I need to know what happened too. I got locked up and accused of a crime I didn't commit. If you know something about that, tell us!"

Lily opened and closed her mouth. "I could get into big trouble for this. Even I have a boss!"

"Just tell us," I demanded.

Lily hesitated then blew out a breath. "Olivia wasn't on the list the day she disappeared, but that doesn't mean she's not dead. People die whether they're on the list or not. And I haven't seen her on the other side either." Lily grabbed some more biscuits and shoved them into her pockets. "Take my advice and stay the hell away from that mess."

"What mess?" I furrowed my brow. "What else do you know? I'm so sick of people keeping things from me!"

Lily shook her finger at us. "The mess your sister got involved in. One man is dead. Liv's gone. Lucy almost got killed and dark things keep appearing. You kids need to leave this alone."

"What else do you know?" Lucy demanded. "Who took me? Who killed that elf? Why —"

"Leave it alone," Lily told her then turned to me. "Be careful working with the Elhanan. They don't mess around." She grabbed a few more cookies. "No more summoning spells either. I have a job to do. The dead can't wait forever." She vanished in a whirl of smoke.

"Lily! That's not fair. You could've told us more." Lucy stamped her foot. "She always does that." She frowned at me. "You're working with the Elhanan?"

I gritted my teeth. That reaper had a big mouth. "Kind of. I'm trying to find my sister. I need to know what happened."

"So do I." Lucy clenched her fists. "I need to know why some bastard took me and possessed me. If you're working on that, then I don't have a problem sharing the dorm with you."

"This won't be easy."

"I know that, but I need to know what happened to me."

"I'll tell you what I know. Which right now isn't much."

Lily nodded. "We'll find out what happened. I know we will."

CHAPTER 11

CASSIE

I awoke to the sound of screaming and bolted up in bed. At first, I thought it'd been me. Ever since Liv had vanished I'd been having nightmares about it. Of Liv being ripped away from me and not being able to reach her. For once, sweat didn't coat my forehead and my heart didn't race like it normally did.

Murphy grumbled from his hammock. He usually came over to comfort me when I had nightmares. But I hadn't been dreaming. Or at least I didn't think I had.

No, it hadn't been me. I'd been asleep, not dreaming for once.

So who had screamed?

A cry echoed down the hall.

Lucy.

I scrambled out of bed and hurried down the hall to her room. I walked past that weird wall again. Static crackled against my skin. I'd have to figure out what it meant later.

Lucy lay in bed with her duvet tangled around her and thrashed around. Her room had beige washed walls like mine. Books were stacked on her desk and there didn't seem to be a thing out of place.

"Lucy?" I called out. "Are you okay? Wake up, you're dreaming." She continued to thrash. "Lucy!" I reached out to grab her and she lashed out at me. "Lucy, stop." I grabbed her wrist, but knew I had to be careful. She screamed again. "Lucy, it's me Cassie."

Her eyes flew open and widened. She gasped for breath and drew away from me. "What are you doing in here?"

"I heard you screaming. Are you okay?"

Lucy ran a hand through her long hair and grabbed her glass of water, then gulped it down. "No, I'm — I don't want you in here."

"Okay. Guess you didn't mean what you said earlier." I turned to leave. Just when I thought we'd made progress.

Her breath came out in pants. "No, I don't want anyone seeing me like this."

"Why? I have nightmares nearly every night." I pushed my hair off my face. "You don't have to hide anything from me. I'll make some tea."

I headed to the small kitchen area which consisted of a mini fridge and a kettle and boiled the kettle. Mum always made tea when people got upset. Not sure if it really helped, though. I fumbled around in the box of teabags Mum had packed in with my stuff.

I headed back to Lucy's room with a mug. "Here, it's chamomile. Supposed to soothe nerves and stuff."

"Thanks." Lucy sniffed. "I'm sorry."

I waved a hand in dismissal. "Don't worry about it. I don't mind."

"Not for the screaming. For what happened to your sister."

"Oh. Right. You don't have to keep apologising for what happened. It wasn't your fault." I believed that. Maybe part of me had blamed her at first but she was a victim too. Someone had used her to bring something dark into the human realm. And I'd damn well find out who it was and why they'd done it.

"Isn't it?" Lucy pulled her knees up to her chest. "If I'd been stronger, maybe —"

"You can't change what happened and it wasn't your fault. You are just as much a victim as my sister. But I will find out who did this to you and Liv."

Lucy sipped her tea. "How do you deal with the nightmares? Where did you get the teabags from?"

"My mum thinks of everything and packed them for me." I slumped onto her desk chair. "It's hard. I keep seeing Liv calling out to me, but can't reach her."

"I keep seeing that shadow thing." She shuddered, put the mug down and pulled her knees up to her chest. "I don't even know what it was and it continues to haunt me."

"They're called shadowlings. I encountered them in Elfhame when I found Murphy." Murphy flew into the room and settled on my lap where he curled up in a ball. He closed his eyes again.

Lucy motioned to the sleeping dragon. "Is he your pet now?"

"Not exactly. He's my best mate." I grinned down at him. "Even if he is trouble at times."

Murphy raised his head and flew over to Lucy. He sniffed at her as he settled on her lap.

"He's so cute." Lucy beamed as Murphy snuggled against her. "Wow, he purrs like a cat. I never expected a dragon to be this tame. Aren't they supposed to be ferocious fire breathers that decimate cities? Although he looks too tiny for that."

"Yeah, he purrs a lot. Don't worry, he won't hurt you. He's a big softy. You can keep him with you for a while if you want."

"You won't mind?"

I shrugged. "Murphy does his own thing."

I headed back to bed and rolled over. Sleep soon dragged me under. This time I didn't find myself back in the warehouse like I normally did. Instead, I found myself in a dark room.

Voices murmured but I couldn't make out what anyone said. Shadows danced along the wall. A scream tore through the room and blood dripped onto the floor in front of me.

When I jolted awake again sunlight streamed in through the window and my alarm buzzed. I hit the snooze button and pushed my damp hair off my face. Holy crap, what had that dream been about? Weird, it felt so real. So familiar. Normally I dreamt of Liv.

Why had I dreamt that? Was it real or just a nightmare?

Glancing at my schedule, I groaned. My first lesson, the fundamentals of magic. Then training with Ash. Oh joy.

After I showered and dressed in my usual

jeans, T-shirt and leather jacket, Lucy and I headed down to the common area for breakfast with Murphy.

The common area was a large hall not far from the great hall filled with dozens of tables. There was an area at the front where different machines dispensed drinks and food.

Lucy found a small table in the corner and settled there. A few disapproving gazes came our way and curious ones when they spotted Murphy with me.

To my relief they also served steak so I ordered a few for him. Murphy's eyes widened in delight and he soon started gobbling down the meat before I even had a chance to take it over to the table. I put the plate of stakes down then went back to get my own breakfast and grabbed some toast and jam.

Before I had a chance to join Lucy, Smiley and his cronies all crowded round her.

Not again.

"Murderers don't deserve to eat our food." Smiley grabbed Lucy's plate.

Murphy stopped cramming food into his mouth, rose into the air and roared.

Smiley and his cronies laughed. "Do you really think a little dragon is gonna scare us?" Smiley made a grab for Murphy, then yelped when Murphy clamped his teeth around the guy's fingers.

"Did I not kick your arse hard enough yesterday?" I headed back over to the table. I moved my plate over to one hand and light formed in the other.

Lucy shot to her feet. "Cassie, don't." She took a deep breath. "I'm not a murderer. I was cleared of all charges. Leave me the hell alone!"

"You're still a murderer. We all know you did it." Smiley gave her a shove, then sneered at me. "You won't be there to protect her forever."

"Maybe I should blow up something else this time." The light in my hand burned brighter.

To my surprise, Smiley and his cronies backed off and finally left.

Lucy breathed a sigh of relief. "They're never gonna leave me alone, are they?"

"They'll move on when they have something else to gossip about. Just ignore them."

"I'm not good at defending myself the way you are. Good thing I signed up for self-defence class. Looks like I'm going to need it."

"Don't let them get to you. We both know you're innocent."

She shook her head. "Yeah, but no one else believes it, do they? You don't have to keep defending me. I don't wanna put you in the line of fire."

"I can take care of myself." I settled down on the bench next to her and Murphy resumed his stake feast. "Don't let them get you down either. I'm surprised they even care about Jared given what he was." I knew elves well enough to know that they hated necromancy. It was something that was outlawed, not only by them, but all supernaturals.

"What's your first class?" Lucy wanted to know.

"Magic fundamentals. Sounds boring."

"I have that too. Sounds fascinating. If we get stuck, we can ask my girlfriend for help."

"Girlfriend? Oh, you mean Evie? She's Silvy's friend." I remembered seeing Evie when I had visited Lucy in prison. I knew Evie in passing from my time at Everlight Academy but I'd known Silvy's family for years.

"Yeah, she's my girl." Lucy grinned. "I wouldn't have met her if I hadn't gone to prison and…" Lucy bit her lip. "Sorry."

"Stop apologising for everything. If something good came from this whole mess, that's great." I spread jam over my toast and took a bite.

"I can't help feeling guilty." Lucy's shoulders slumped.

"We all have guilt. You just have to deal with it and enjoy the good things you do have. That's why my mum says. Can't say it's working very well for her, though."

"Hey, Cass!" Mike bounded towards us.

"Ooh, he's fit." Lucy grinned.

"You have a girlfriend."

"I do, but that doesn't mean I can't still admire other people."

Mike came over.

"Hi, Mike."

Murphy, who sat on the table gorging the rest of his steaks, growled when he saw Mike then huffed out a plume of smoke.

"Why does he keep doing that?" Mike frowned.

I shrugged. "No idea. Maybe he's not used to you yet."

"Or maybe he's jealous because you're male." Lucy chuckled. "He's probably not used to men being around Cassie."

"Why would he need to be jealous?" I snorted. "We're just friends. Luce, we'd better get to class."

"Hey, can we hang out later and catch up?"

Mike asked.

"Maybe. My schedule is pretty full right now."

Mike's face fell. "Oh, okay. Right."

Lucy and I headed off. "What was that about?" she asked.

"What?" I stared at her in confusion.

"Mike is into you and you just blew him off."

I laughed. "Mike and I broke up months ago." I pulled out my map. "Any idea where the Forest of Beasts is? I'm supposed to drop Murphy off there since he's not allowed in class with me."

"Guess we'd better find out. You should take Mike up on his offer."

I frowned at her. "Mike and I are better as friends. I don't have time for romance right now."

"Or do you like that hunky elf?"

"Ash? Goddess no! He's so annoying and so not interested in me."

We walked along the path and came to a large standing stone with symbols on it.

"Hey, I think this is one of those teleportation things," Lucy said. "They can transport us from one part of the island to another."

"How does it work?"

"We tell it where we want to go and it takes us there."

"Okay, Forest of Beasts." I touched the stone and bright light flashed around us.

Murphy screeched as me and Lucy stumbled headlong into a tree. Murphy leapt into the air and I put my hands out to steady myself.

"Okay, are we in the right place?" I shoved a branch out of the way before it hit me in the head. "Would it kill the elves to put a few signs up to tell us where the heck we are?"

The trees stood like silent sentinels around us. A heavy canopy of green and brown. We pushed our way through the trees until we came to a clearing. Murphy flew around in excitement and made chirping sounds.

"Says here I'm supposed to meet Mara." I glanced at my paperwork again.

"That's me." A woman with bark-like skin, wearing a green dress, dark hair and glowing green eyes appeared. "You must be the girl they told me about."

I'd never seen a dryad up close before. There weren't many in the human world. "Hi, I'm Cassie and this is…" I glanced around and frowned. *Murphy, get over here!* A blur of light bounced around the trees and Murphy jumped into my arms. "This lunatic would be

Murphy."

"Goddess, a firedrake." Mara beamed. "They're very rare. Most were hunted to extinction over the last few centuries. Many supernaturals fear dragons and don't appreciate them being the incredible, majestic beasts they are."

Firedrake. I already knew that from my research but hadn't found out much more. I'd been too focused on finding Liv.

"Where did you find him?" Mara asked as Murphy fluttered around her. "I haven't heard of any of these being seen in two hundred years. It's very unusual for them to bond with anyone. You must be very special indeed."

I hesitated. I hadn't told people much about Murphy because I feared someone would take him away. Something had guided me to Murphy and told me to protect him. So I'd done that.

"I found him whilst travelling. You sure he'll be okay here? We've never been apart for long." I still didn't like the idea of leaving him for several hours. But I knew he'd wreak havoc being stuck indoors for so long. And I couldn't take the risk of him disrupting class.

"Of course. We have some other dragons here that he can play with. Dragons need the companionship of their own kind so there's no need to worry about him."

Murphy flitted around Mara like they were old friends.

Maybe I'd find the separation harder than he would.

CHAPTER 12

CASSIE

Lucy and I headed for our first class at the Magical Arts Tower. This tower looked very different from the enforcers tower. It stood at an odd angle almost like the leaning Tower of Pisa. It was made out of golden sandstone and had glittering diamond pane windows.

A tall old man with a long white beard and pointy ears stood at the front of the class. He reminded me of the humans' idea of a wizard. Not what I expected.

I took a seat next to Lucy since she was the only one who didn't send glares my way.

"Welcome, class. I am Engelbart Nolan but you can call me Bert. Today we're going to be going over the fundamentals of different magic systems. Including elves, fae, witches and shifters."

"Shifters have magic?" a female elf at the

front of the class scoffed.

I recognised her as the bitchy girl who'd egged on the elves yesterday when Lucy was terrorised.

Who is she? I asked Lucy in thought.

Oh, that's Elora Elmese. She's a niece of the Elven Queen. Best not to piss her off.

"All supernaturals have magic to some degree. Even shifters."

"Shifters are nothing but filthy beasts." A gorgeous male elf next to Elora sneered. "Why are we even talking about them? They don't have magic."

"Actually shifters are very powerful since they can take on two forms *and* wield magic," another girl said. She had long red hair and black wings so I knew she had to be fae. She had a weird aura of power around her.

Who's that? I asked Lucy.

Ivy Blue. She's half fae, half witch. Spends a lot of time experimenting with different magics. Real social outcast. The elves are scared of her and everyone calls her Ghost Girl.

Why?

Because she's like a ghost. We lived in the same group home together. She always seemed to disappear like a ghost. Lucy shook her head. *She's a little weird. Talks to her cat a lot rather than people.*

Hey, I walked around with a baby dragon.

Who was I to judge? A pit formed in my stomach at the thought of Murphy. I kind of missed the feel of his presence. Guess I got more attached to him than I expected.

Ivy's name sounded familiar. I'd heard of her when I have gone to Lucy's group home after Liv disappeared. She'd been one of the people there who had refused to cooperate with me. All she had said was Lucy was trouble.

"Now with fae magic, all of their gifts come from the elements. Most fae can wield one or two elements. It's rare for them to wield more than one but Silvana Goodwin, the fae queen, is one such fae," Bert told us. "Elven magic is very similar. It comes from nature and the elements as well. We can wield more than one element and between elements. Does anyone know what a between element is?"

I thought this class would be easy since I'd learnt fae magic growing up. I had learnt about other magics from Mum. She travelled around a lot when she was younger and met a lot of supernaturals. I got my love of travel from her.

I hated to think how lonely she might be now. She still hadn't dealt with Liv being missing. Instead, she'd gone into a weird grieving/trying to be normal phase. I didn't know how she'd deal with me being gone but at the same time we needed a break from each other. That didn't mean I wouldn't miss her, though.

Ivy raised her hand. "In between elements are an extension of the five elements, earth, air, fire, water and spirit. In between elements are lightning, light. Ice and turbulence."

That made sense.

"Good, Miss Blue. We'll be doing a few tests."

The teacher rambled on about differences in magic systems.

"Mr — Bert." I hated how awkward I sounded. "What about wild magic?" I'd seen the term in my textbook with a warning label attached but no explanation. And it brought up things I hadn't thought about in a long time. Wild magic came out of the Nether Realm.

Elora snorted. "The fae half breed doesn't know what wild magic is."

I know way more than you think. Someone needed to bring up the subject.

"Hush, Elora." Bert frowned at her. "Wild magic is something that surrounds Elfhame and the Nether Realm. It's an uncontrollable force."

"That's not true," Lucy spoke up. "Slayers were supposed to control it."

I flinched. Holy crap, did she know what I was? I had mentioned working with Ash, not the slayer part.

Elora cackled and tossed her long hair over her shoulder. "Slayers are myths. They're just something told to scare kids. Like a bedtime story."

Great, I'm a bedtime story.

"There's a lot of truth in myths," I pointed out. "Maybe you don't know the slayer because you haven't seen one for a while."

"Right, keep on dreaming, faeling."

Elora wanted to piss me off but I ignored her. Heck, I'd been called worse.

The rest of the class passed in a blur.

"What's your next class?" Lucy asked as we headed we left the Magical Arts Tower. The spiral steps were narrow and portrait of different elves hung along the sandstone walls.

I glanced at my schedule. "Training with Ash near the forest. That's vague."

Lucy grabbed my map. "That's where my self-defence class is. Maybe we have another class together."

"Hey, what do you know about slayers?" I

asked out of curiosity. "I didn't think anyone outside of the elven world knew about them."

Lucy arched a brow. "What's with the sudden fascination with elven warriors?"

I shrugged. "I'm just curious."

"They're like fey guardians. Only they didn't have their powers imbued in them by witches. They were a bunch of elven warriors," Lucy explained. "They had supernatural strength, speed and senses. They could wield magic too. But they're said to have been wiped out. Some people say the Elven Queen destroyed them because they were a threat."

"I thought one survived? She died about seven years ago." I knew I had to be careful about what I said about Estelle. I didn't want Lucy to figure out who and I was.

Lucy shook her head. "I don't think so. It'd be cool if one did survive. They stopped things that came from the Nether Realm. Like the Elhanan do. Slayers were said to be the best. They had the strength of true elves."

"But how do you know about them?" My mind raced with questions.

"I read a lot. Especially stuff about history and different supernatural creatures. That's why I want to get my degree and become an analyst for the Elhanan. Or at least I did. I'm not sure they will accept me now. Not after I was arrested for murder."

"But you were pardoned."

Lucy rolled her eyes. "You know what the elves alike. They don't forgive or forget. Most of them still think I'm guilty."

I couldn't argue with that.

Defence classes were in a small redbrick building near the herbalism forest. Its whitewashed walls and shiny floor made it look very new compared to most of the buildings I'd seen so far. A few mats covered the floor along with weapons and other equipment hanging on the walls.

"Wow, this place looks intense," Lucy remarked. "I only wanted some self-defence skills. I know I'll probably be needing them."

"Don't worry, you'll be kicking arse in no time." It'd help if Lucy knew how to defend herself better. I knew I couldn't always be there to protect her

To my horror, Elora and some of her cronies also came in. Great. Just great. I thought Elora would be too afraid to break a nail to go near weapons.

"Oh, goody." Lucy groaned when she spotted Elora. "Maybe I should consider private lessons."

"Ignore them. The taunting will die down

once they get something new to fixate on." I tied my hair back into a messy ponytail.

"What's more shocking than murder?" Lucy hissed.

"We both know you're innocent. That's all that matters."

"Easy for you to say. You're not on their radar."

"Don't be so sure of that." I glanced at my watch. "Ash is supposed to meet me here, so where is he?"

Ash himself then came in. "Morning, class. Everyone ready to get started?" He flashed everyone a dazzling smile.

"Whoa, he's the teacher." Elora put her hand on her chest. "Goddess, am I drooling?"

I rolled my eyes. Sure, Ash might be gorgeous but he didn't impress me. His smile wouldn't make me go weak at the knees.

I didn't know whether to be annoyed or relieved our training session wouldn't be one-on-one as I'd expected. He gave us a quick rundown on what we'd be doing in class. Then he'd test us all one by one to see what abilities we had.

He started going over the basics and how defence came from the body (end) magic. I wondered if there was any point to this whole process.

What happened to us training together? He was the one who insisted (that) I needed training again — despite training to be a slayer from the age of four. I might have stopped seven years ago but I hadn't lost all of my skills.

Did Ash really think I needed self-defence skills? I hadn't lost my skills in that department.

Guess I would just have to prove that to him.

CHAPTER 13

ASH

I focused on the class and didn't let my attention wander over to the slayer. We'd have to wait to start training until after this class. I had agreed to teach self-defence and weapons training. I already graduated from the academy last year so I didn't have study to worry about. I shared the role with my friend, Tye.

"First up, I want to show you some basic defensive moves. I need a volunteer."

"I'll do it." Elora stepped forward and her friends all giggled.

By the nether, why did it have to be her? I knew Elora had a thing for me but she was too much of a princess for my taste. Pretty but no substance. I liked a woman who could handle herself. Not one who wanted to act like a damsel in distress.

"Okay, one common way for an attacker to grab you is in a chokehold." I wrapped my arm around Elora's neck. "Elora, how would you fight me off?"

Elora just stood there for a moment and pressed her body closer to mine.

"Elora, you need to focus here."

Cassie sniggered.

"I guess I could scratch you and scream."

"I can easily cut off your scream." I put my hand over her mouth for good measure.

Elora flailed about and waved her arms. I tightened my hold on her. "You need to do anything you can to get your assailant to let go before they render you unconscious." After a while, I let Elora go since she didn't seem to be making much effort. "Anyone else want to volunteer?" I glanced around.

"I'll do it." To my surprise, Lucy stepped up.

I caught her in a chokehold. "Okay, how —?"

She elbowed me in the ribs and I gasped, surprised from the blow.

"Was that good?" She bit her lip.

"Yeah, that was." I nodded. At least she had some fight in her. "Okay, everyone partner up and I need someone else to volunteer to work with me. Someone who already knows her stuff." I gave the slayer a pointed look. "Cassie?" We may've been apart for a few years but she knew how to fight and would at least know the basics.

Lucy's eyes widened and she gave Cassie a shove forward. "Go on. This could be fun. Show everyone how it's done."

She sighed and stepped up as I did a quick run through of what people should practice.

"Thought we were training together?" Cassie whispered.

"We are, one-on-one after this class. Right now I'd like to assess your skills."

"You can't assess me like this." She scoffed. "This stuff's child's play. I learnt about chokehold's and kicks over a decade ago. You know I can fight."

I grinned. "Okay. Let's go. Show me what you got, slayer."

Cassie snorted. "There's no way you could handle me."

I arched a brow. "Cocky, I like that. You too afraid to show me your moves? Been a while since we sparred together."

"As if." Cassie took off her hoodie and tossed it aside.

The girl had a muscular, curvy body. One you didn't get from the gym. Damn, the girl looked fine.

"Come on then." She splayed her feet.

"Listen up, class. You're about to see a real fight," I told them. "Well, maybe." I took a fighting stance too. "Give it your best shot."

Cassie threw a punch. I turned my head and raised my hand to block her next blow.

I moved so fast she didn't have time to react as I caught her in a chokehold and wrapped my free arm around her stomach and immobilised her arms. "You're holding back," I whispered. "Don't."

"You sure about that?" Cassie sneered. "Like I said, you can't handle me."

"Try me. I won't hold back if you want." I couldn't deny I liked the feel of having her close.

She flashed me a smile and head-butted me, stomped on my foot. I winced, then she pulled me over her shoulder and threw me to the ground.

I landed hard. Damn, the girl still had a lot of strength.

"Now that's how to break a chokehold." Cassie put her hands on hips.

I sprang up. *Okay, slayer. You're on.* I flew at her.

She dodged my first blow, spun and scissor kicked me. Cassie moved with the grace of a true fighter. She hadn't lost the training she'd had when we were kids. She moved and knew how to anticipate my moves.

I didn't hold back this time. I used my full strength to fight back but I didn't want to hurt her. We were having fun. If she really wanted to take me down she could have. And vice versa. I couldn't remember the last time I had someone who could match me to spar with.

People cheered as I went for a final blow the Cassie kicked my legs out from under me, jumped on me and pinned me down.

"If you wanted to be on top, all you had to do was ask." I laughed at my joke.

"Get your mind out of the gutter, Ash." Cassie moved away from me and sprang up. She stalked off and went to re-join Lucy.

I spent the rest of the class showing them different moves and getting everyone to practice their defence techniques.

I made Cassie work with me a little bit more. I could tell she wasn't happy about it but how were elsewhere we going to get used to working with each other again? Besides, she was too skilled to be practising basic moves.

"Okay, class over." I rubbed my now-aching jaw. Damn, the girl hit like a hammer.

"Yeah! You kicked arse, girl!" Lucy high-fived her. "Ready for the next class?"

"Yeah, it's here."

Tye came in and drew me to one side. "Whoa, you let the half breed wipe the floor with you, bro. What gives?"

I thumped him on the shoulder. "Don't call her half breed. That's racist. She is half elf." As I was only half elf, I hated being judged because of it.

Tye arched a brow. "I didn't mean it like that. You don't fancy her, do you? You already have a girl."

"Risa isn't my girlfriend. She's a friend with benefits. I didn't let Cassie wipe the floor with me."

"Someone must have trained her pretty well."

I nodded. "I'll see you later. I've got training today."

"Wait, is that the —?"

"Keep your voice down," I hissed. "You can't go around telling people what she is."

"Aren't you at least gonna introduce us? I'm dying to meet her."

Cassie waved at Lucy then headed back over to me. She hooked her thumbs in the pockets of her jeans. "Now what?"

"Cass, this is Tye. He's an enforcer too."

Tye held out his hand. "It's great to finally meet the infamous Cassie. You should know he never stops talking about you."

Her eyebrows rose but she didn't take his hand. "Really? Why's that?"

"Probably because you were his best friend growing up. Don't think he's ever forgotten about or got over losing you." Tye drew his hand back to look offended by her not taking it. He flashed me a grin. "You two have fun now. See you later, Ash."

He strode off before I could say another word. Unbelievable. I couldn't believe he'd said that to her face.

The class trailed off, leaving me and Cassie alone. "I see you've still got the moves." I smiled at her and brushed off my embarrassment.

"I didn't give up fighting just because I moved away, Ash." She crossed her arms. "You still talk about me?"

"Yeah, you are my best friend. Then you have a think about me over the years?" I wasn't sure I wanted to hear the answer to that but I said it anyway.

"Maybe. Please tell me will be doing some better training than basic self-defence moves. Doing that is a complete waste of time. I'll never get back into the rhythm of being a slayer if we go back to kid stuff."

I had to admit she did fight much better than I'd expected after being out of the game for so long. Maybe her slayer skills weren't as rusty as I'd expected. At least she had stayed in shape and her reflexes weren't bad either. But her magic needed the most work.

"Can we go for a walk?"

She narrowed her eyes. "What about training?"

"Training can wait a bit longer."

"Okay, I guess."

We headed out to the nearby the port. The sea breeze blew Cassie's hair across her face as we headed along the dock.

"Do you remember Prithya? The city that bordered Elfhame and the human realm. You know the one there's all the legends about."

"We used to live there when we were kids. I don't remember that much about it." She furrowed her brow. "Why do you ask?"

"Do you remember much about what happened to Estelle?"

"Not really. Mum — Nina didn't tell me much but I know something bad happened to her." She shook her head. "I try not to think about it. I'm not sure I want to remember what happened that night."

"Estelle never seemed to be around much. She left you alone or asked my dad to watch you most of the time. She loved you but I think she changed a lot towards the end. I think she got involved with someone bad and they killed her."

"Maybe it's better not to remember. I'm not sure I want to know what they did to Estelle. I know it's bad." She reached under her jacket and clutched something. The necklace I'd made for her. It looked like an intricate siler Celtic circle.

"I can't believe you still have that." I smiled. "Do you remember how you got it?"

"You said was a magical amulet and would always keep me safe." Cassie smiled too. "I remember that. I never take it off."

It felt good. Almost like we were kids again. As much as I wanted to trust her, we weren't kids anymore, though. We'd both changed. "I hope we can be friends again."

"I hope so too," she agreed.

CHAPTER 14

CASSIE

Reminiscing with Ash about being kids had thrown me a bit. I had a lot more questions.

I touched my necklace. Weird, I never took this off. I knew it probably wasn't magical but somehow I thought it always kept me safe. It always been special to me.

"Where have you both been?" Cal paced up and down as Ash and I headed back to the classroom. "We have important training to do." He glared at Ash. "You know that."

"Sorry, Cal. We've just been catching up. And I've been testing her skills. She can still fight pretty well."

"And I can kick his arse." I grinned.

"A slayer, much like the Elhanan, checks things that come through from the Nether Realm. The nether exists between this world and another dimension."

"I already know what it is. A place of unimaginable evil — that's what Estelle always used to say."

"Not all of the Nether Realm is a place of evil. It's a realm and home to many different creatures like the Ever Realm and Elfhame."

"There's good and bad in every world. But bad things do come from Nether." Ash crossed his arms and leaned against the wall.

"There's something I need to show you. We're going to teleport to the northern point of the island." Cal held his hands up to me and Ash.

I hesitated. "What is it?" Father or not, I wouldn't be quick to trust this man.

He might be Ash's mentor but I didn't feel a connection to him the way I did with Ash.

Ash grasped Cal's arm and I grabbed the other arm. Light flashed around us.

We reappeared on what looked like an empty patch of grassy field. The white lighthouse and the port stood in the distance. I let go of Cal and he walked off, then raised his hand. A wave of glowing light flashed front in of him. "This boundary wards the island. Beyond it lies the wild magic and the Nether."

Wild magic. I heard about the growing up

with Estelle. I knew it was bad.

"Right. It comes from the Nether Realm. It's uncontrollable."

Cal nodded. "Indeed. The boundary is to hold it back but often it leaks through. That's another duty of the Elhanan — to keep it under control so it can't harm others." Cal reached out and pushed through. "All enforcers can get through the boundary in case we need to force the magic back or if anything comes through." He motioned for us to follow. "Come. As my daughter, the magic won't repel you."

Great, he just had to mention that again!

Ash followed suit. I hesitated. I didn't like the idea of walking through a wall of energy. What if I got stuck or knocked on my arse?

I took a deep breath and walked through.

On the other side stood an area with more grass and beyond that lay thick sparkling fog.

"This marks the edge of the island where the nether begins." Ash motioned towards the fog.

"Slayers can control the magic wild magic to an extent" Cal took off his jacket. "That's why I want to test your powers myself now. Raise your hands and see if you can push the wild magic back. I need to see how uncontrollable your powers really are."

I really didn't like the sound of that. Wild magic was unpredictable. After not training for so long, how did he expect me to be able to push back wild magic?

"I used some pretty strong magic yesterday when I saved Lucy. I think I felt some wild magic around me then."

"What were you feeling?" Cal frowned.

I shrugged. "I don't know. Annoyed, I guess. They were gonna stone Lucy."

"Your power reacts to your emotions. Let's get started. I want you to concentrate on opening a portal."

"Just raise your hands and concentrate, like you did in class," Ash told me.

A chirping sound made me look up as light darted through the boundary. Murphy leapt at me.

"Hey there, matey." I grinned and caught hold of Murphy. "Boundaries are no match for him either."

"Concentrate, Cassie."

"Go, Murph."

Murphy flew over to Ash and greeted him in excitement. Weird, he never acted that way around anyone else. It seemed they were best mates already.

I raised my hands and willed my light magic to appear.

Nothing happened.

I tried again.

Nothing. Not even a flicker of light.

"Try to focus on what you felt yesterday," Ash suggested. "Concentrate."

I thought about how angry I'd felt when Lucy been tormented. Light sparkled between my fingers and fizzled out.

"Perhaps you're not a slayer after all. Your mother could use magic better than anyone," he said. "You couldn't even save your sister, could you?"

What the fuck?

I raised my hands and knocked Cal off his feet. I gasped in shock.

He laughed. "Not what I expected but good. Your mother's powers reacted to anger too."

"Try again." Ash put his hand on my arm, his body hard and warm on my back. "Focus on what you want to happen. You can do this."

"Yeah, how would you know?"

"Because I seeing you do it before. Just because you walked away from your old life doesn't mean that knowledge and skill isn't still inside of you."

I tried to ignore the feel of him being close. Odd, a feeling of comfort came over me.

More power crackled between my fingers again. I closed my eyes and let instinct takeover.

"Concentrate, Cassie. You'll never be a slayer if you don't learn to focus," a woman's voice said.

Where had that voice come from? It almost sounded like my birth mother, but that was impossible. Or maybe it had been a memory.

When I opened my eyes again, Ash had moved away and a swirling portal hovered between my fingers.

I gasped. "Now what do I do?"

Light shot into the wild magic as though it'd been sucked through a giant vacuum.

"Good, now let go." Cal's voice sounded urgent.

I dropped my hands and gasped again. It felt like all the air had been sucked out of me.

"You are off to a good start." Cal touched my shoulder. "But your magic is very unpredictable. That was just a simple test. Nothing like what a real slayer would have to face in battle."

I couldn't believe I had heard my birth mum's voice. I hadn't thought about her that much over the years. Part of me hadn't wanted to revisit that painful time in my life. But things changed. I'd changed for one thing.

"What happened the night my mum Estelle was killed?"

Cal and Ash glanced at each other.

"Something came through from the Nether. It broke into your house and killed her." Cal's expression turned grim. "Things have changed over the past few years. More creatures are coming through the nether than ever before. Something seems to be banding them together."

"Like what?"

Cal shook his head. "We don't know but our job's more crucial than ever."

"Has anyone ever been into the Nether Realm to find out?" That seemed like the logical thing to do. How could they fight something if they didn't know what it was?

"Travel into the Nether Realm's impossible. We've sent people before but none have ever come back no matter what we tried."

"People can't communicate with us in the nether either," Ash said. "That's why we can't find out much of anything."

"That was a good start," Cal said. "We just need to be ready for whatever happens next."

CHAPTER 15

CASSIE

So I survived my first day of classes and training when I headed back to my room that evening. Murphy drooped on my shoulders. Frolicking in the forest all day had worn him out. I felt tired too.

After practising the wild magic, I endured a couple of hours of sword lessons and other training with Ash. Along with history and potions classes. I was ready to drop. I forgot how exhausting school and slayer training could be after not attending or practising in years.

I barely felt like eating dinner in the common area. Ash had sat with me. It felt good hearing stories about our childhood. Now all I wanted now was a hot shower and then chill for the night.

"Whoa," I said as I walked in.

Lucy had somehow had more furniture moved in. I had no idea where got it she'd from. Her girlfriend had something to do with it I guessed. But we now had a small settee and TV in our tiny living area.

"Hey, did you leave your wet towels on the bathroom floor?" Lucy frowned from where she sat on the leather sofa. "I know we're roommates but you could at least pick up after yourself."

I yawned. "What towels? I haven't showered since this morning."

"Well, I haven't showered either. So who else could have been in there?" Her frown deepened. "Does Murphy shower?"

I snorted. "No, he hates water and he cleans himself." I glanced at my paperwork. "It does say we have another roommate." I had found it weird how the housing office said I'd be with two people.

"There's only two rooms plus this area and the bathroom."

I thought back to that weird wall at the end of the hall. That had given me a strange vibes.

"Maybe it's here and we haven't seen it." I shoved Murphy off my shoulders and headed into the hallway. Lucy and Murphy trailed after me.

"There's nothing here." Lucy shook her head.

"Someone must've used those towels." I pulled out a pen and threw it at the wall. It bounced off something that flashed with static.

"What the hell is that?" Lucy asked.

"I don't know. Maybe a ward." I reached out and more static charged against my fingers. "There's a door here but I can't see any way to open it."

Lucy raised her hand and threw a fireball at the door. Sparks exploded everywhere and the door burst open.

Lucy and I stuck our heads through. The room looked around the same size as mine. Except alchemical charts and bookcases covered the walls. The desk had books and papers all over it. A duvet covered the bed with a large pentacle on it. A black cat lay on the pillow.

A redheaded girl looked up from her desk. "Hey, what are you doing?" she demanded. "Did you try and blow my door off?"

Lucy narrowed her eyes. "Ivy. I should've have known. It's polite to introduce yourself when you live with someone."

"I don't live with you. Now get out of my room!"

"You're using our bathroom. That means you our roommate." Lucy scowled. "Can you learn to pick your towels up off the floor?"

"Why did you hide your door?" I asked Ivy.

"Because I want to be left alone. Get out!" Ivy waved her arms. "I'll complain to the housing office. I can't believe they put me in with the sister of a murderer and a convicted criminal."

"Hey, I'm not criminal. I was cleared of all charges." Lucy growled at her.

Lucy, chill, I told her. *Let me talk to her.*

Why?

Because you two seem to rub each other the wrong way.

Lucy gritted her teeth. "Don't touch my stuff either." She stomped off.

"Look, maybe we got off on the wrong foot. I'm —" I stopped when Murphy flew in and jumped on the bed beside the cat.

Ivy yelped. "Keep that thing away from my cat!"

Murphy brushed against the cat, who purred loudly.

"It's okay. He's just saying hello."

"Stop that beast from coming in here." She grabbed hold of Murphy and shoved him towards me. "Make sure he stays out. I'm not here to make friends, I have work to do."

"Okay." I headed out and her door vanished again. "I must find out how she does that."

Murphy squealed and looked back at the door. "Sorry, matey. Ivy doesn't want to play nice."

"I don't want her here," Lucy growled. "I'm not a criminal! She's a freaking nightmare. She has a criminal record too — and she's actually guilty."

"She does seem kind of prickly. She freaked out when Murphy went near her cat." I snorted. "He loves animals. He likes making friends."

"I'm going to the housing office first thing."

"We've only been here a couple of days. Don't you think we should try and get along with her? Sounds like she'll keep to herself anyway."

Lucy blew out a breath. "Fine, but she'd better keep her judgement to herself."

Lucy and I spent the next couple of hours going over our classes for the week.

"I thought college was supposed to be easier than school?" Lucy groaned.

"They just say that to make you spend more on tuition.

"What's the deal with Ivy?" Lucy lay

sprawled on the floor with her books and tablet out. "I only heard rumours of about the kind of trouble she got into when we lived in a group home. I heard she stole things and broke into her father's lab."

"I can find that out easy." I tapped a few keys on my laptop. "Here we go…Ivy Blue. She's eighteen and her parents died in an accident several months ago. Academically she looks awesome but she also has a sealed juvenile record."

Lucy's mouth fell open. "How did you find that out so fast?"

"I didn't get my PR licence for fun. I've been running background checks from my mum for years."

"What's her sealed record about?" Lucy got up and sat next to me on the settee. "Can you view it?"

I hesitated. "Maybe we shouldn't."

"Don't you want to know if our roommate's a psycho?"

"If she was, she'd probably have more than a juvenile record." I clicked on the sealed record which flashed with "restricted" on screen. "The fae seal their records with only minimal security. Here we go."

An image of Ivy appeared on screen. "What are those different place names?" Lucy frowned

"Those are magical research centres. Says here she broke into them and stole different substances."

"Great, we're living with a junkie."

"I don't think so." I scrolled through the text. "Says here she took different things with really long weird names. But I don't think they're drugs."

Lucy grabbed a pen and scribbled the names down. "I'll find out what they are. But first I have a date. Don't wait up for me."

"I won't."

I scoured through Ivy's record further. It seemed like she had a pretty sad life after she lost her parents. She had no surviving family. Some of the things she'd stolen were experimental magical substances. Some were experiments to bridge the gap between life and death. Others were supposed to bring the dead back to life. She wanted to bring her parents back. I couldn't blame her for that. Ivy wasn't a psycho. She just didn't have anyone left.

An explosion shook the air and the walls vibrated.

"What the hell?"

Murphy yelped and flew off the top of the sofa where he'd been snoozing. He made a few clicking sounds of annoyance.

I put my laptop down where I switched to looking through Elhanan files.

Murphy and I hurried down the hall. Ivy's door stood wide open and visible.

"Are you okay?" I coughed and couldn't see through the haze of smoke.

Ivy coughed and groaned. "Damn, that should have worked!"

"Where are you?" I couldn't make out much through the smoke.

"Get out. I told you to stay out of my room!"

"Yeah, well, that was before you nearly blew up half the building." I narrowed my eyes and spotted her on the floor. Grabbing her arm, I yanked her up. "Are you hurt?"

"No, this wouldn't have happened if that stupid housing place—"

"Oh, sure, you could kill only yourself then." My voice dripped with sarcasm. I went to the window and yanked it open. "You're not testing chemicals in here to raise the dead, are you?" I muttered the fae word for clean and a gust of wind blew through the room and cleared the smoke.

Ivy doubled over coughing. "How — do you —"

"I'm a PI. I'm good at finding things."

"Those records are sealed. No one is —" She gritted her teeth. "I'm not trying to bring my parents back. I tried a new experiment. I'm trying to get degree in magical metaphysics but no one give me the space to conduct my research. That's why I need my own space."

"I don't think conducting experiments in your dorm room is a good idea. Don't you need a controlled environment for that?"

"My room has pretty strong ward around it." Ivy groaned at the sticky substance that covered her top and skirt. "And I'd love a controlled environment but they won't let me have one. Please, don't spread rumours about my record. It cost me a fortune to even get a place here."

"I don't spread gossip. And for the record, Lucy didn't kill anyone and nor did my sister. Do you think I'd live with Lucy if she had?"

"How'd you know? You weren't there."

"I helped her to get out of prison."

"Why?"

"Because the fae queen and I proved she didn't kill the elf."

"Fine. Whatever. I've never had someone freak out over towels on the floor before."

"I think she's a neat freak."

"Argh, my experiment is ruined."

"What was that stuff?"

"Primordial dust. It's to create solid matter from energy." Ivy put her hand over her mouth. "Shit, I shouldn't be telling you that."

"Ivy, what you do in your spare time is your business." I raised my hand. Light sparked between my fingers and all of the black stuff shot into a jar. "That's new."

"How'd you do that?"

"No idea, I was just gonna cast a spell to get stuff off you."

Ivy smiled. "Thanks. You're my saviour. My Alchemy professor will kill me if I lost all this stuff."

"Please promise you'll practice with this stuff somewhere else."

Ivy nodded. "I will. I don't want to get kicked out because of blowing up a building." She sighed.

"I'm sure there's someone else."

"Maybe… Thanks. For your help, I mean."

"No problem."

Maybe I had broken the ice with her at least.

CHAPTER 16

CASSIE

The next few days passed in a blur of classes and training. I was glad when the weekend finally swung around again.

Ash and I hadn't had much time to go over Liv's case because I'd been so busy with classes and slayer stuff. But Ash was coming over so we could finally go over things. I convinced Lucy to stay awhile so she could go over what she remembered. Just in case I'd overlooked something.

Ivy seemed to have warmed up to me a little. She and Lucy still bickered a lot.

"I still can't believe you invited Ash around here on a Friday night to discuss murder." Lucy pulled her long brunette hair up into a high ponytail.

"Why? Should I have waited until

tomorrow?" I arched an eyebrow at her. "Plus, we want to know who framed you for murder."

"Of course but don't you want to be alone with him?" She waggled her eyebrows at me.

"Why would I want to be alone with Ash?"

Lucy snorted. "Look, I get you want to find Liv but Ash is gorgeous and perfect for you."

"I barely know him and I thought you were gay? If you like Ash so much you date him!"

Lucy grinned. "Even I can appreciate good looking man. Right, Ghost Girl?"

Ivy glared at her. "I'm not a ghost, fairy."

"Well, you sure as hell go around invisible a lot." Lucy returned her glare.

"I like it. Saves me having to talk to annoying —"

"Ivy, why don't you do whatever you have planned for tonight?" I waved her away.

"Right. I'm not allowed in your little crime club." Ivy scowled and tossed her long red hair over her shoulder.

"You can stay if you want to hear about the case. I didn't think solving a murder was your thing."

"It's not." She stalked off.

"Could she get any weirder?" Lucy rolled her eyes.

"Ignore her. I have your case files all

ready."

"You're not gonna wear that, are you?" Lucy motioned to my clothes.

I glanced at my T-shirt and jogging bottoms. "What's wrong with these?"

"Nothing be you look like a messy pile of laundry."

I sighed and hurried back to my room. I ran a comb through my hair and put on jeans and a clean purple shirt. "Better?"

"A bit. But you could try something sexier."

I threw a cushion at her. "I'm not interested in Ash."

"Why?" Ivy poked her head around the corner. "Even I have to admit he's like a wet dream."

"Yeah, there's so much chemistry between you," Lucy added. "Or do you want Mike again? I see the way he looks at you."

"Would you both please stop? I'm not interested in Ash. How many times do I have to tell you both that?" I threw my hands up in exasperation. "Now give it a rest or I'll slay both of you."

Lucy snorted. "I have fire."

"I have magic too and enough explosives to destroy the entire island," Ivy protested.

"You really are a freak," Lucy sneered.

A knock came at the door.

"That's Ash. You two learn to be civil for a while."

They both sneered at each other and I hurried off to answer the door.

Ash had on his usual black jeans, dark shirt and leather jacket. Looking sexy as sin. "Hi." He flashed me a smile.

I flushed and wondered where that stray thought had come from. "Hi." I gave him a wry smile. "Come on in."

"Where's my favourite dragon?" Ash caught hold of Murph and fumbled in his pocket for something. "I bought you some treats."

Murphy wolfed the treats down.

Both my roommates peered around the corner to gawp at him.

"Er... Lucy wants to hear about the case too. This is Ivy."

Ivy grinned. "Hey."

"Don't you have poo to play with?" Lucy prodded her in the ribs.

Ivy turned red. "It's primordial — never mind." She stormed off. Lucy chuckled.

"I've got the case files." Ash held up a folder.

"Oh, I have them already."

His eyes widened. "You do? How —" He

sighed. "I'm not gonna even ask."

"It's better if you don't, trust me." Lucy perched on the beanbag whilst Ash and I took the settee. "Have you got any new leads? Like who was held at the house when I was held captive there."

"No, there was no trace left at the scene. Whoever was there covered their tracks pretty well." Ash shook his head. "The whole team went through the scene again but there's nothing there."

I groaned. "So we've basically got nothing?"

"Weren't there are any witnesses?" Lucy demanded. "Someone must have seen something."

"It was the middle of the night and that house was shielded," Ash replied. "Now I'm technically not the investigator in this case but I've gone over everything more than once. Lucy, I'd like you to meet with a seer. One who is gifted at bringing out repressed memories. Would you consider going to see her?"

Lucy's mouth fell open. "Are you joking? Of course I'll see her. Duh, I want to find the bastard who framed me for murder. When can we go?"

"Tomorrow, if you want. But this isn't

something to be taken lightly. Vinessa is... Pretty intense. There's no telling what she might bring up."

"I'll do it."

Lucy stayed for a while whilst we talked about the case and eventually left to go for her date night.

"Cal would probably kill me if he knew I was letting Lucy be involved in this." Ash shook his head. "I might as well throw the rule book out the window."

I scoffed. "Rules are there to be broken."

"You haven't changed much." He laughed. "Just like the time you talked me into taking your mum's car for a joyride. I thought she was gonna skin me alive."

"You? I thought she would crucify me. Why didn't you say no to me?"

"Come on, Pratley I worshipped the ground you walked on. I would have done anything for you and you know it." Ash furrowed his brow. "Wait, you remember that?"

I nodded. "Yeah, we had a blast. Well, before my mum tracked us down."

"My dad hit me pretty good that day too."

"Where is your dad? I have a few vague memories of him. Didn't he play the piano a lot?"

"Yeah, but I don't where he is now. We had a falling out a few years ago."

"I'm sorry."

"It's okay. I went to live with Cal after that. He's been like a dad to me."

I sighed. "I wish I could remember more."

"Maybe you can. I know a spell that we use on witnesses to help them recall memories. Wanna try?"

I hesitated. "We should try it on Lucy."

"It didn't work on her."

"Okay, how does it work?"

Ash laced his fingers through mine. "I'll chant the spell. Just close your eyes and focus on what you want to remember."

I tried to ignore the warmth of his hand in mine. My roommates'd made me feel weird around him. Sure, he might be gorgeous but I wasn't interested any kind of romance.

Ash chanted a few words in a strange language I recognised as old elvish.

Energy crackled between us as I closed my eyes. I thought about the night the warehouse and found myself back there.

"Wait, stop!" Lucy told me and Liv. "You don't understand."

"We understand. We're taking you into custody." Liv took my cuffs from me. "You can tell the elves everything you know."

"But —"

An explosion ripped through the air. My eyes blurred and a ringing sound went through my ears.

The image changed and I was somewhere else. Huddled in a corner. Screaming echoed around me for so long I covered my ears. When I couldn't take any more. I crawled out from my hiding spot. A dark figure had a woman on the ground.

My mum. Estelle.

She kicked the figure away and reached for her sword. "Cassie, run!" she yelled at me. "Get somewhere safe."

I gasped as my eyes flew open and tears streamed down my face.

Ash let go of my hands and gripped my shoulders. "What did you see?"

"The warehouse then... My mum. I distracted her. What if —"

Ash wrapped his arms around me and pulled me close. "Hey, it's okay. You didn't cause her death. It was only a glimpse of a memory."

"You don't know that."

"I do. Your mum was strong. It would take more than that to bring her down." He ran a hand through my hair.

I cried against his shoulder and he just held

me.

"You used to hold me like this when we were kids."

His lips curved into a smile. "Yeah."

I laid against him. It felt good to be close to someone.

He didn't push me away either. I wouldn't have blamed him if he did. The last thing men wanted was a woman sobbing all over them.

Finally sleep dragged me under.

CHAPTER 17

ASH

Something licking my face dragged me awake the next morning. Golden eyes met mine.

Murphy.

It took me a second for me to remember where I was. Cassie lay asleep against my chest. Someone had put a blanket over us.

"Get off me, Murphy." I waved him away and hated to think of a dragon looking me. Murphy bounced onto Cassie, who still lay against me asleep. "Murphy, go," I hissed.

I didn't want to wake her up. Maybe I should have left last night but it had felt good being close to her. I couldn't remember the last time I'd been close to anyone. Not with Risa at least. We had sex. We didn't snuggle like this.

I glanced at my watch and it revealed it was gone seven. I couldn't believe I'd stayed all night. Maybe I should leave now.

"Murph, get off me!" Cassie groaned and her eyes widened when she spotted me. "Ash, what are you doing here? Did we —" She pulled away.

"We fell asleep together." I rubbed the back of my neck. "I should go."

"There's probably a good idea." Her cheeks flushed.

I stood up and grabbed my jacket.

Murphy pounced on me again, making clicking sounds. "Is he like this every morning?" I frowned.

"Yeah, it means he wants breakfast." Cassie pushed her hair of her face. "Come on, Murphy."

"Er — I'll see you later. When I come to take Lucy to see the seer."

"Right. See you then."

As I went down the hall, Cassie's roommate arched an eyebrow at me but said nothing. Now I felt awkward. But we hadn't done anything.

I teleported back to my flat and found a pair of woman's shoes by the front door. Risa. Crap, I'd forgotten we were supposed to hook up. I found her laying on my sofa fast asleep.

"Risa?" I shook her shoulder.

She jolted awake, her long black hair over her face. "What the fuck, Ash?" she snapped. "I can't believe you left me alone all night."

"I'm sorry. I got caught up."

She jumped to her feet. "Why do you smell like that new girl you've been working with? I can smell her all over you."

"I fell asleep with her. That's all." She took a swing at me but I caught hold of her arm. "Risa, I swear nothing happened."

"I see the way you look at her."

"She's my oldest friend. And if something did happen you're not my girlfriend."

Her dark eyes narrowed. "Did you want something to happen?"

I blew out a breath. "I never said that. Would you please go? I need a hot shower. I have stuff to take care of today." I pulled off my shirt and kicked off my shoes. Tugging off my jeans and boxers, I let the hot water flush wash over me. I needed to get the smell of dragon off me.

My front door slammed shut as Risa stormed out. I couldn't imagine why she thought I was interested in Cassie. Yeah, I cared about her but we could never be more than friends.

I went back to Cassie's room later that morning to get her and Lucy. Dread filled me at the idea of seeing Vinessa. The woman was odd but she had power. Power to give answers.

I knocked on the door and Lucy answered it. "Cassie's coming." She pulled her hair back into a ponytail. "Do I look okay?"

I glanced at her flowery dress. "I guess. The seer won't care if you dress nice or not."

"She's elven, right?"

I nodded.

"Then I look good. My girlfriend told me elves are insulted if —"

"Most elves aren't sticklers for the rules." I glanced behind her. "Where's Cassie?"

"Oh, she went off to take her dragon to the forest and make sure he has enough food whilst we're gone. I swear she babies him too much."

I told her not to bring Murphy. Vinessa might not react well a mysterious dragon. She'd probably consider him a weird omen or potent.

Light flashed as Cassie reappeared. "Hey, ready to go?" She wore her usual jeans, T-shirt and jacket.

We headed out to the island's largest

standing stone. It could transport people between the realms. Vinessa lived in Elfhame. This stone was one of the few that could transport people back and forth. The island had it so students could travel back and forth with ease.

An odd buzzing sensation washed over me as I walked through the portal. On the other side, cracks of sunlight came in through the thick canopy of trees.

"Whoa, that was weird." Cassie stumbled into me.

"Argh, I feel sick." Lucy covered her mouth.

"It will wear off. You just need to get used to it," I told them. "Vinessa's house isn't far. Let's go." Leaves crunched under my boots as I headed up the trail.

Cassie kept pace with me whilst Lucy trailed behind.

"Be on your guard around Vinessa. She can be... Intense."

"Intense how?" She furrowed her brow.

"Well, sometimes she states stuff that you didn't want to know." I rubbed the back of my neck. "And she —"

Murphy blurred over our heads in a flash of light. He wrapped himself around Cassie's neck.

Lucy groaned. "Can't we go anywhere without him?"

Cassie shrugged. "He doesn't like it if he can't sense me."

"Okay, why is he on me?"

"Maybe he thinks you need him."

Murphy purred against her.

"Cass, your dragon thinks he's a cat."

Cassie and I headed on whilst Lucy grumbled to Murphy.

"As I was saying, Vinessa —" I stopped when my senses prickled.

Cassie froze and glanced around. She must've sensed the warning on the air.

"Both of you run ahead to the house. You'll be safer there. Tell Vanessa I sent you," I hissed.

Murphy hovered beside Cassie as Lucy took off running.

"What is it?" Cassie asked.

"Never mind, just go."

"I'm the slayer and we're supposed to be partners. I'm not leaving you." She crossed her arms. "So tell me what it is."

"My guess would be shadowlings."

A shadow shot towards me. I raised my hand and blasted it with a beam of light. It screeched as the light tore it apart.

"That was easy," Cassie remarked.

"That wasn't a shadowling. It was an underling spirit. They use them to scout ahead."

More wailing followed.

"So light kills them?" Purple light sparkled between her fingers.

"Light slows them down. Only a portal can banish them."

"Which you can open, right?"

"If the wild magic doesn't interfere, yeah, but if not... Portals aren't easy to open if you're a long distance from the Nether."

Even though I'd trained as a magus I still struggled with portal sometimes.

More shadows darted above the tree line.

"Screw that, let's go." I grabbed Cassie's arm and we ran.

One shadowling shot in front of us and slashed its talons at Cassie, grazing her arm.

She flinched. Murphy flew overhead. Light shot from his mouth and exploded a shadowling. Then another.

Cassie and I both threw bursts of light.

Murphy clamped his teeth on another shadowling and used light from his body to destroy it.

I raised my hands to conjure a portal. Gold light flashed between my palms. Cassie gripped my wrist and her power flowed into mine. The portal expanded.

"We need to force them through." I gritted my teeth as I struggled to keep the portal open.

"Leave it to me." She pulled away and threw another burst of light at the shadowlings.

All of them swarmed towards her.

I fuelled more power into my portal.

Murphy roared again. His body still glowing as he shot towards Cassie. He landed on her shoulder. One by one shadowlings shot through the portal.

I gasped for breath as the portal closed.

"Well, guess I got my perfect taste of being a slayer." She winced to clutched her arm.

"Here, let me heal that. Shadowlings carry poison so it's important to heal any injuries you get from them." I held my hand over her arm. Light radiated over her until the poison was gone. I brushed my fingers over her skin and pushed the hair off her face.

Our eyes locked for a moment. "You've — you healed me before, haven't you?" She furrowed her brow.

"Yeah, that's what a magus does. We're there to help the slayer."

She shook her head. "No, I meant before now. When we were kids."

"Yeah. Come on, we need to get moving."

CHAPTER 18

CASSIE

I rubbed my arm. Not because it hurt anymore but because I could still feel the warmth of Ash's touch on my skin. I'd seen a brief flash of Ash healing me. But when had it been? What had it been for? Ash hadn't given me any details either. I tried asking but he said we needed to check on Lucy.

A house loomed up ahead made of weathered grey stone. With a thatched roof and wooden shutters.

Why anyone would want to live in a dark forest like this was beyond me. It was creepy as hell.

Murphy wrapped himself around my shoulders and Lucy sat on the step waiting.

"Why didn't you go inside?"

"Because you didn't tell me your friend was

—"

The front door creaked open. A hag with long straggly grey hair and only one eyeball peered out. The other eye socket remained empty. The remaining eye appeared milky white. She wore a long black robe and pointed ears peeked out through her straggly hair. She reached out.

Lucy ducked out of reach. "Are you sure we're at the right place?" she whispered.

"Vinessa." Ash stepped forward.

The hag reached out and ran her gnarled hands over his face. "Ashland Rhys. It's been a long time."

"I told you to call me Ash. No one calls me Ashland."

Lucy came over to me. *Please don't let her touch me. Why didn't he warn us about her?*

You shouldn't judge someone by the way she looks, I pointed out.

Yeah, but the smell —

"Hi, Vinessa. We need your help with something. A case."

She ran a hand down his chest. "Your heart feels lighter somehow."

I wondered what the heck she meant by that.

"You know my visions come with a price, boy." She ran pointed nail down his chest.

"Wait a minute, what price?" Lucy demanded.

Vinessa moved past Ash and walked right up to Lucy, who ducked behind me.

Vinessa ran her gnarled hand over my face. "Well, well, a slayer. I see you found your girl, Ashlan. Didn't I tell you you would?"

"Yeah, you did." Ash rubbed the back of his neck. "And I'll pay whatever price is required."

"Interesting, very interesting. You have a lot of power, girl. Your past and future are shrouded in shadow."

I shoved her hand away. "Hi, I don't like being touched. And I'm not the reason why we came to see you."

"Come inside." She reached around me, grabbed Lucy's arm and yanked her towards the house.

Guess we were going in.

What price? I asked Ash in thought. *What do you have to pay her?* I didn't know if he would hear me or not but I didn't usually have trouble talking to people telepathically. Plus, I figured as we had talked to each other as kids then we might still have a mental link.

He shook his head. *Not with money. She always asks for something in return.*

Like what?

I favour. An item. Whatever she feels like.

Inside the house didn't look much better.

Candles flickered everywhere. A table with two chairs sat in the centre of the room. A rickety-looking wooden sofa with threadbare cushions stood against the far wall. Ash and I headed over and sat down on it.

Lucy sat down on one chair and picked at her nails.

Weird-looking crystals hung from the ceiling, sending waves of dancing light around the shadowy room.

Vanessa sat on the other chair.

Murphy flew across the room and grabbed hold of one of the dangling crystals.

The elven seer shot to her feet. "Stop that!" Vinessa barked and grabbed hold of him. She ran her hands over his small body. "A firedrake. Well, I haven't seen one of these in a generation. You need to learn some manners, boy."

Murphy blew out a plume of smoke then shot over to me and Ash. He wrapped himself around my neck.

"What do you want to know?" Vinessa stared at Lucy with her milky eye.

"To — to know who framed me for murder. To know who killed that elf and why. Who else was at that house with me?"

"That's more than one question." She turned her head towards Ash. "Are you willing to pay such a price?"

"Just find out who else was at that house that night." Ashe waved his hand in dismissal. "That's what we came to find out."

"Very well, give me your hands, girl." Vinessa held out her gnarled palms.

"Wait, what's the price?" Lucy glanced from the seer and back to Ash. "I need to know."

"I want a favour. You agree to that, don't you, Ashlan?"

"I already agreed to that." Ash crossed his arms.

Lucy still hesitated then took Vinessa's hands.

What kind of favour are you gonna give her? Is she really going to help us?

He shrugged. *She sees a lot more than she lets on. As for the favour, I have no idea. It could be anything.*

Wait, she said you found me. Did you look for me after Estelle's death?

Ash hesitated. *Yeah, I needed to know what happened to you after your mum died. I — I needed to know you are okay.*

Okay. I blew out a breath. I didn't know how to feel about that. How far had he gone to find me? I meant to ask him but Vinessa's energy jolted through the room. Maybe I could peek in and see what she saw. *Wanna be sneaky with me?* I held my hand out to Ash. *I might be able to see her vision.*

She won't like that.

Suit yourself.

My eyes snapped shut but Ash laced his fingers through mine. The vision dragged us both in.

Lucy found herself back in the cage. Someone else sat in the second cage behind her but they were hidden by shadow.

Jared stood in front of an altar and chanted to spell. Shadows merged around him. One shot straight into Lucy.

Someone screamed and the second cage blew apart. Footsteps echoed as someone ran away.

"No!" Jared yelled. "Come back here!" Then he screamed and silver light flashed as someone slashed him with a knife.

I gasped as the vision faded.

Lucy panted, sweat broke out across her forehead. "Why can't we see more? I need to know who was there."

"Whoever was there cloaked themselves somehow." Vinessa let go of Lucy's hand.

Ash shot to his feet and gave Lucy a hand

up. "Come on, I'll get you back to the stone."

"Good, that was creepy as hell." Lucy shuddered.

I realised Murphy had vanished again. "I'll be right behind you," I told him. "Murph, where the hell are you?" I half expected him to appear.

Vinessa's creepy gaze followed me around the room.

"Murphy, come here!" I put my hands on my hips.

No sign of him on any of the hanging crystals. I heard a scrambling sound and hurried into the next room.

Murphy had his tail hanging out of a wooden box as he rummaged through it. "Stop that!" I hissed and yanked him out. "Are you tryna get us in trouble?"

Something shiny dangled from his mouth. I gasped at the heart-shaped pendant. *Liv's necklace.*

Crap. How had that gotten here?

A lump formed in my throat. If I'd been there or bothered to answer her calls, I would have answers. I'd know what had been going on in her life.

I took the necklace out of Murphy's mouth and headed back out with him on my shoulder. "Why do you have my sister's necklace?" I held it up. For all I knew she could see it.

Vinessa rose and hobbled over to me. "I keep people's secrets." She yanked the necklace from my grasp.

"But you met her, right? Her name's Olivia Morgan."

"I can read you if you want the answers you seek, slayer. You want to find your sister and know why you can't remember much of your past."

My mouth fell open. "How the hell do you know that? Can you read my thoughts?"

Vinessa chuckled. "No, but I can sense things. Let me read you. I will give you the answers you seek."

I turned to leave then hesitated. "You didn't give Lucy much of an answer," I muttered.

"The answer is right in front of you."

I furrowed my brow. If it were, then I had no idea what the answer might be. "Can I have my sister's necklace? I gave that to her."

Liv had loved that necklace. I couldn't believe she'd given it up to anyone.

"What will your price be?" Murphy curled himself around my shoulders. "Oh, and he's not included in any deal."

"If you promise me a favour, I'll give you

answers."

"Enough with the cryptic crap. I'm not Ash. What would this favour involve? I want specifics."

Yeah, I wanted to find my sister more anything but I wouldn't be stupid enough to lose something valuable to this sneaky woman.

"This reading I will do for free."

I narrowed my eyes. "Why?" Nothing in this world ever came free. And if it did there was usually a catch.

"Your mother helped me a long time ago. I owe her a debt." She held up her hand.

I hesitated. Would this be worth it? Would she give me answers?

Murphy, off. I tapped him and he flew up into the rafters.

I grasped her hand. Energy vibrated between our palms. Her eye blazed with light.

I closed my eyes and I found myself back in the warehouse. I found Liv lying on the ground, then it changed to her and Jared arguing. I couldn't make out what they said.

"You were supposed to help me," Liv snapped. "You promised me."

"It's not my fault I can't find her. I told you, piercing the veil isn't easy," Jared snapped back.

"I want results. I need to find her." She glanced over at the altar. "What are you doing?"

"I'm gonna summon some spirits who will be able to help get us more answers." He cupped her chin. "Hey, I want to find her as much as you do."

She scowled when he kissed her.

The vision faded and my head spun. "Who was she looking for?" I clutched my head and swallowed the bile in my throat.

"That answer will come in time." Vinessa kept hold of my hand. "Now are you ready to see your past?"

"Wait, I thought you said one favour."

"Consider this part of the favour. You intrigue me, slayer."

"I doubt one vision is gonna show me everything I want to know."

"We shall see."

I sighed and nodded.

Her eyes flared with light again.

The vision dragged me back under. This time images blurred by so fast I couldn't make out anything.

Energy crackled between our joint hands. Vinessa screamed and my eyes flew open. Light pulsed between us and burned through Vinessa's hand.

Crap! I yanked my hand away and weird symbols flashed over palms.

What had I done?

CHAPTER 19

ASH

"You okay?" I asked Lucy.

She rubbed her arms up and down. "Creeped out. That's one crazy hag."

"She's not bad. She's just... Intense."

"Why couldn't I see the other person who was there?"

"Visions can't answer everything. They only give us clues."

"Sorry, Obi-Wan. But I need real answers."

I snorted at the Star Wars reference. "Answers take time."

"Yeah, well, forgive me for wanting to know why I spent two long months in prison." She sighed. "It must be worse for Cassie, though."

"I'll do whatever I can to help."

"You really care about her, don't you?"

Lucy frowned. "I mean, I know you were friends as kids but —"

"Yeah, I do. But we can only be friends. There are rules about slayers and magi."

Lucy snorted. "That's... Archaic."

"Rules are there for a reason." I'd never been one for breaking the rules. Not like Cassie. She'd always break rules when we were kids. I doubted now would be any different.

"You can't deny you two have chemistry."

I froze as my senses prickled with a warning and a chill ran over me. Something was wrong with Cassie. "Lucy, get through the stone. Now!"

She frowned. "Why?"

"Just go!" I sprinted back towards Vinessa's house and burst through the door.

Vinessa lay slumped in the chair. "Don't touch me," she hissed when Cassie reached for her.

"What in the nether happened?" I glanced between them. Given Cassie's panic I'd expected something to have attacked them or worse.

Cassie had grown pale. "She — she had a vision and I burned her. Vinessa, I'm so sorry. I didn't mean to." She glanced at her hands. "I don't know what happened."

"Your memories are cloaked." Vinessa

used her other hand to conjure a bowl of water. She dipped her burnt hand into it.

"Cloaked?" She furrowed her brow. "Why would anyone do that? *Who* would do that?"

"Your mother, no doubt." Vinessa scowled.

"But why? Do you mean Estelle? Or Nina?"

"Your true mother. And I don't know why she would do it. To protect you perhaps."

"Protect her from what?" I went over to the table. "Here, give me your hand. I can heal you."

Vinessa drew back. "Your magic may not work on me." She bandaged it with a piece of rag. "Both of you need to leave. Now."

Cassie and I headed out. "Why would Estelle cloak my memories?"

I shook my head. "I don't know. None of this makes sense." I stopped. "What price did she ask you?" I shouldn't have left her alone with Vinessa. Vinessa would have loved the chance to get her hands on the slayer and see her future. But I thought Cassie had been right behind us like she'd said.

"Vinessa said she'd do this reading for free. Said she owed a debt to Estelle."

My eyes widened at that. "Vinessa never does anything for free."

"Do you think she lied to me?"

In truth, I couldn't be sure. Maybe Vinessa had just wanted to use her powers. I had seen how eager she was when she first touched Cassie. She probably had worked with Estelle.

"I don't know. Maybe not. Let's get out of here."

We made our way back to the stone.

I wanted somewhere more private where we could talk without fear of being overheard.

Risa wouldn't be in my place but I didn't feel right. "Want to see something cool?" I asked and held out my hand.

"Okay."

We reappeared on top of an old tower. It was a small tower that had once been used as part of the island's military base but it hadn't been used in years.

"What is this place?" Cassie furrowed her brow.

"It's an old disused tower. They renovated it a few years ago but haven't decided what to do with it yet. I come up here to think sometimes." I pulled a couple of deckchairs out from behind the chimney. "Have a seat. What else did Vinessa say?"

Cassie slumped onto the chair. "Liv wasn't just sleeping with Jared. I saw them arguing on the day she disappeared. She was angry because he hadn't found someone for her."

I took out my phone and wrote down some notes. "What else did you see?"

"Liv said Jared hadn't found whoever she was looking for." She shook her head. "I can't imagine who she'd want to find."

"Could she have meant you? You were off travelling."

"Liv could have found me without sleeping with Jared."

"Has she lost anyone? What about someone in her personal life? Or maybe your birth mother?"

Cassie hesitated. "I don't think so. I know she had a girlfriend but she's still very much alive. I still can't fathom why she'd be involved with Jared. As for our mum, no. Why would she need to look for Estelle? She died years ago." Murphy settled on the arm of the chair next to her.

"What did you see when she looked at your past?"

"I didn't see anything. Just a blur of images that didn't make any sense." She shook her head. "Then I somehow burnt her. Why would Estelle cloak my memories?"

"Maybe she didn't want you to remember something. It could be anything."

We sat and went over the case files again. I

put up a ward to stop the wind from coming near us or the files.

"We know Olivia was working with Jared so she could find someone." I marked out a flowchart. "Was she in love with Jared? We ruled that out as unknown because Jared was a ladies man. We found evidence of Olivia being in that house before the day she disappeared."

"She was there? Weird. She never mentioned that when we went to the house." Cassie sighed. "There's so much I didn't know about her life."

"Even the people closest to us keep secrets. If Olivia was there, then did she see Lucy and whoever was with her?"

"Maybe we should go to the club where Liv worked. The people might know something."

"Cal and I already interviewed everyone there when we looked into Olivia's — disappearance." I avoided saying death since it would upset her. "We never got much from anyone. I couldn't find any close friends of your sister either."

"She wasn't close to many people. Back when her music first took off a lot of people messed about with her. It was just us after Estelle's death so we were each other's rock."

"If she wanted to find someone, who else

would she have told?"

Cassie bit her lip. "Other than me? Mum would be the only other person she'd trust."

"Maybe you should call her and ask. See what she knows."

"Mum and I haven't talked much since I came to the academy." She took out her phone. "Hey, Mum. It's me. Are you free to talk?" She put it on speaker phone so I could hear.

"Cassie? Finally! I've been so worried. Are you okay? That bloody Elhanan haven't —"

"I'm fine. Mum, we found out Liv was searching for someone. That's why she was with Jared." The line went silent several minutes. "Mum, are you still there?"

Nina blew out a breath. "I know she was looking for someone but I couldn't find out anything else. Have you looked at the enforcers' sealed files?"

"Mum, there are no sealed files. I could unlock them in my sleep if they were. Believe me, then it. So don't bother lying to me."

The line went silent again.

"Why couldn't you tell me any of this before?" Cassie demanded.

"Because I didn't want you chasing down dead ends. Liv's not coming back."

"That's not true. Why did Estelle cloak my

memories?"

"That's what I'd like to know." I leaned back in my chair. "I know Cassie got injured when her mum died."

"I did?" She frowned at me.

"Yeah, you had head trauma."

"Mum, why didn't you tell me any of this?" Cassie demanded.

"Because I want the past to stay buried. I don't know who Liv would be looking for. You need to stop chasing after this because you're not going to find anything."

"I have to go." Cassie hung up before Nina said another word.

I reached out and took Cassie's hand. "It'll be okay."

"Will it?" She rubbed her temples. "Because I think everyone is keeping stuff from me."

I pulled her in for a hug. She didn't move for a while.

Maybe I wasn't supposed to get involved but I couldn't stand seeing her hurting. My files fell to the floor and scattered.

Cassie sniffed and pulled away. "Sorry."

"No worries." I bent to pick them up. One of them was a photo of Jared. "Maybe the answer to all of this isn't about Liv. Maybe it's him."

CHAPTER 19

ASH

"You okay?" I asked Lucy.

She rubbed her arms up and down. "Creeped out. That's one crazy hag."

"She's not bad. She's just... Intense."

"Why couldn't I see the other person who was there?"

"Visions can't answer everything. They only give us clues."

"Sorry, Obi-Wan. But I need real answers."

I snorted at the Star Wars reference. "Answers take time."

"Yeah, well, forgive me for wanting to know why I spent two long months in prison." She sighed. "It must be worse for Cassie, though."

"I'll do whatever I can to help."

"You really care about her, don't you?"

Lucy frowned. "I mean, I know you were friends as kids but —"

"Yeah, I do. But we can only be friends. There are rules about slayers and magi."

Lucy snorted. "That's... Archaic."

"Rules are there for a reason." I'd never been one for breaking the rules. Not like Cassie. She'd always break rules when we were kids. I doubted now would be any different.

"You can't deny you two have chemistry."

I froze as my senses prickled with a warning and a chill ran over me. Something was wrong with Cassie. "Lucy, get through the stone. Now!"

She frowned. "Why?"

"Just go!" I sprinted back towards Vinessa's house and burst through the door.

Vinessa lay slumped in the chair. "Don't touch me," she hissed when Cassie reached for her.

"What in the nether happened?" I glanced between them. Given Cassie's panic I'd expected something to have attacked them or worse.

Cassie had grown pale. "She — she had a vision and I burned her. Vinessa, I'm so sorry. I didn't mean to." She glanced at her hands. "I don't know what happened."

"Your memories are cloaked." Vinessa

used her other hand to conjure a bowl of water. She dipped her burnt hand into it.

"Cloaked?" She furrowed her brow. "Why would anyone do that? *Who* would do that?"

"Your mother, no doubt." Vinessa scowled.

"But why? Do you mean Estelle? Or Nina?"

"Your true mother. And I don't know why she would do it. To protect you perhaps."

"Protect her from what?" I went over to the table. "Here, give me your hand. I can heal you."

Vinessa drew back. "Your magic may not work on me." She bandaged it with a piece of rag. "Both of you need to leave. Now."

Cassie and I headed out. "Why would Estelle cloak my memories?"

I shook my head. "I don't know. None of this makes sense." I stopped. "What price did she ask you?" I shouldn't have left her alone with Vinessa. Vinessa would have loved the chance to get her hands on the slayer and see her future. But I thought Cassie had been right behind us like she'd said.

"Vinessa said she'd do this reading for free. Said she owed a debt to Estelle."

My eyes widened at that. "Vinessa never does anything for free."

"Do you think she lied to me?"

In truth, I couldn't be sure. Maybe Vinessa had just wanted to use her powers. I had seen how eager she was when she first touched Cassie. She probably had worked with Estelle.

"I don't know. Maybe not. Let's get out of here."

We made our way back to the stone.

I wanted somewhere more private where we could talk without fear of being overheard.

Risa wouldn't be in my place but I didn't feel right. "Want to see something cool?" I asked and held out my hand.

"Okay."

We reappeared on top of an old tower. It was a small tower that had once been used as part of the island's military base but it hadn't been used in years.

"What is this place?" Cassie furrowed her brow.

"It's an old disused tower. They renovated it a few years ago but haven't decided what to do with it yet. I come up here to think sometimes." I pulled a couple of deckchairs out from behind the chimney. "Have a seat. What else did Vinessa say?"

Cassie slumped onto the chair. "Liv wasn't just sleeping with Jared. I saw them arguing on the day she disappeared. She was angry because he hadn't found someone for her."

I took out my phone and wrote down some notes. "What else did you see?"

"Liv said Jared hadn't found whoever she was looking for." She shook her head. "I can't imagine who she'd want to find."

"Could she have meant you? You were off travelling."

"Liv could have found me without sleeping with Jared."

"Has she lost anyone? What about someone in her personal life? Or maybe your birth mother?"

Cassie hesitated. "I don't think so. I know she had a girlfriend but she's still very much alive. I still can't fathom why she'd be involved with Jared. As for our mum, no. Why would she need to look for Estelle? She died years ago." Murphy settled on the arm of the chair next to her.

"What did you see when she looked at your past?"

"I didn't see anything. Just a blur of images that didn't make any sense." She shook her head. "Then I somehow burnt her. Why would Estelle cloak my memories?"

"Maybe she didn't want you to remember something. It could be anything."

We sat and went over the case files again. I

put up a ward to stop the wind from coming near us or the files.

"We know Olivia was working with Jared so she could find someone." I marked out a flowchart. "Was she in love with Jared? We ruled that out as unknown because Jared was a ladies man. We found evidence of Olivia being in that house before the day she disappeared."

"She was there? Weird. She never mentioned that when we went to the house." Cassie sighed. "There's so much I didn't know about her life."

"Even the people closest to us keep secrets. If Olivia was there, then did she see Lucy and whoever was with her?"

"Maybe we should go to the club where Liv worked. The people might know something."

"Cal and I already interviewed everyone there when we looked into Olivia's — disappearance." I avoided saying death since it would upset her. "We never got much from anyone. I couldn't find any close friends of your sister either."

"She wasn't close to many people. Back when her music first took off a lot of people messed about with her. It was just us after Estelle's death so we were each other's rock."

"If she wanted to find someone, who else

would she have told?"

Cassie bit her lip. "Other than me? Mum would be the only other person she'd trust."

"Maybe you should call her and ask. See what she knows."

"Mum and I haven't talked much since I came to the academy." She took out her phone. "Hey, Mum. It's me. Are you free to talk?" She put it on speaker phone so I could hear.

"Cassie? Finally! I've been so worried. Are you okay? That bloody Elhanan haven't —"

"I'm fine. Mum, we found out Liv was searching for someone. That's why she was with Jared." The line went silent several minutes. "Mum, are you still there?"

Nina blew out a breath. "I know she was looking for someone but I couldn't find out anything else. Have you looked at the enforcers' sealed files?"

"Mum, there are no sealed files. I could unlock them in my sleep if they were. Believe me, then it. So don't bother lying to me."

The line went silent again.

"Why couldn't you tell me any of this before?" Cassie demanded.

"Because I didn't want you chasing down dead ends. Liv's not coming back."

"That's not true. Why did Estelle cloak my

memories?"

"That's what I'd like to know." I leaned back in my chair. "I know Cassie got injured when her mum died."

"I did?" She frowned at me.

"Yeah, you had head trauma."

"Mum, why didn't you tell me any of this?" Cassie demanded.

"Because I want the past to stay buried. I don't know who Liv would be looking for. You need to stop chasing after this because you're not going to find anything."

"I have to go." Cassie hung up before Nina said another word.

I reached out and took Cassie's hand. "It'll be okay."

"Will it?" She rubbed her temples. "Because I think everyone is keeping stuff from me."

I pulled her in for a hug. She didn't move for a while.

Maybe I wasn't supposed to get involved but I couldn't stand seeing her hurting. My files fell to the floor and scattered.

Cassie sniffed and pulled away. "Sorry."

"No worries." I bent to pick them up. One of them was a photo of Jared. "Maybe the answer to all of this isn't about Liv. Maybe it's him."

CHAPTER 20

CASSIE

The next few days passed in a blur of more classes, training and going over the case files. Ash and I dug up everything we could on Jared but so far hadn't found anything.

"Goddess, that was a long day." I pushed my damp hair off my face. "I swear Ash is trying to work me into the ground." Ash had me practising with weapons and magic at the same time now.

"Can we go over the case files again? I want to make sure we didn't miss anything," Lucy added.

"Sure, but we've been over everything. Believe me. I've read them so many times I can probably recite them by now."

"Let's order a pizza too." Lucy grinned.

"Okay, I'll ask Ivy if she wants to join us."

Lucy's grin faded. "Why?"

"Because she's our roommate and it doesn't look like she socialises much."

"I wonder why. Maybe because she's antisocial?"

"Luce, she's been through a lot. Wouldn't it be easier for you two to get along?"

"Sorry, Cass, but I don't like her. Something about her rubs me the wrong way."

"Why?"

"I don't know." Lucy shook her head. "And it has nothing to do with the fact she's a complete slob."

I headed down the hall and knocked on Ivy's door. The door flew open to reveal Ivy wearing goggles and an apron covered in purple goo. "Cassie, didn't I tell you not to disturb me?"

I raised my hands in surrender. "O-kay. Just wanted to ask if you'd any dinner yet?"

"No. I'm busy."

"Lucy and I are getting a pizza. Wanna join us?"

I knew Lucy thought Ivy was a lost cause. Maybe Ivy was prickly but I knew what it felt like to be ostracised and feared. No one deserved that.

"I'm busy," she repeated.

"Can't your primordial goo wait awhile longer?"

She shook her head. "Look, I appreciate you being nice to me but I have work to do."

"Suit yourself. Lucy and I are studying boring case files anyway." I shut the door and headed back down the hall to my room to join Lucy.

We sat on beanbags and placed the files on the floor.

"There must be something here we're missing." Lucy chewed on a strand of her hair. "Someone was in that house with me when Jared took me prisoner. I just know it. There must be something else we can try. Are you sure the Elhanan interviewed everyone?"

"From what I can tell, yeah. My mum and I have pretty extensive files. We talked to everyone that lived on that street."

"Maybe we should talk to them again. Cast a spell on them or something."

"Luce, we can't just cast spells. There are rules."

"You're a PI. I bet you cast spells on people all the time."

"I use my instincts more than anything. I'm usually good at spotting liars."

"Someone must know something. Maybe we should try and contact the spirits. I know that kind of magic is hard but it's possible."

"My cousin Jolie is a medium. I'll call her and see if she'll help."

Jolie had been avoiding me recently. I knew she'd been involved with Jared too. She'd been there with Liv when they'd opened a portal to the Nether Realm.

I took a deep breath. I hadn't told Lucy anything about Jolie's involvement before now but I knew I'd have to sooner or later. It would be better if she heard it from me.

"There something I should tell you. Jolie was there," I admitted.

Lucy narrowed her eyes. "What do you mean?"

"She was there with Liv the night Jared took you."

Lucy's mouth fell open. "Why didn't you mention this before now?"

"Because I needed to be sure I could trust you first. I don't want the enforcers knowing she was there."

"Why not? What was she doing there? How do you know she didn't —"

"Lucy, don't go there. She was just a witness. Jared was teaching her how to use her abilities better. She had Liv with her because Liv wanted to open a portal to the Nether Realm. Don't ask me why because I have no idea." I rose to my feet. "We can go and talk to Jolie again, if you want."

"You bet I do."

Lucy and I headed out to find Jolie.

"Are you sure she can tell us anything?" Lucy asked as we headed into the housing block. "I can't believe she was there." Her hands clenched into fists.

Maybe now hadn't been the best time to tell her but I was glad I'd got it over with.

"Maybe you should sit this one out."

"No way! I want to lay eyes on the person who had me falsely imprisoned." Lucy scowled.

"Jolie didn't kill anyone." If Lucy started accusing my cousin, I knew things wouldn't go well.

"How can you be sure of that? People are always blind when it comes to family."

"Just let me handle this."

I know I should have waited until after I'd seen Jolie to tell Lucy the truth.

Great timing, Cassie.

"You charging and accusing her won't help," I added. "Maybe you should go."

"I thought we were friends?" Lucy crossed her arms.

"You are or else I would have told you

about Jolie's involvement."

Lucy gritted her teeth. "I promise I'll be quiet but please let me go with you."

"Okay, but don't interfere."

I knocked on Jolie's door and we waited.

"Maybe she's not home," Lucy mused.

"She's in there. I can sense her." I knocked again. "Jo, open up. We need to talk.

"Yeah, or maybe we should just call the Elhanan about you," Lucy called out.

"Lucy! Threatening her won't help!"

Lucy scowled. "Are you gonna tell Ash about this?"

I hesitated. As much as I wanted to trust Ash again I didn't want the Elhanan shifting Jared's death unto Jolie. They didn't believe in the whole innocent-until-proven guilty thing. If you were there when the crime took place, that made you guilty.

The door slid open and Jolie's pale face stared back at us. "Come in."

Her room was smaller than my dorm with a single bed, a desk, chest of drawers. Clothes and books were strewn all over the floor.

"I knew you'd come see me sooner or later." Jolie bit her lip.

"What did you and Jared do to me? Did you kill him?" Lucy demanded.

Shit. I should have known Lucy wouldn't

react well to finding out about Jolie.

Jolie flinched. "Of course not. I didn't even know they'd be there. That was all Jared's doing."

"You didn't do anything to stop him though, did you?"

"Lucy." I sighed. "Please just chill out." Magic pulsed from my hand and she froze in place. "Lucy?" I waved my hand in front of her face but she didn't move.

"Goddess, what did you do?" Jolie gasped.

"I have no idea. Must be another sign of my powers advancing. It should wear off soon." At least I hoped it would. "You need to tell me what else you know."

"I already told you everything." Jolie threw her hands up in exasperation. "I worked with Jared since I summon spirits. And before you ask, no. I can't summon Liv. Believe me, I've tried."

"Wait, you have?"

"Yeah, I couldn't find her on the other side."

"So you agree she's not dead?"

Jolie shrugged. "I can't be sure."

Lucy unfroze again. "What do you know?" she asked Jolie.

"She says she's not sure if Liv is dead." Good. That gave me hope. "Jo, why did you,

Jared and Liv try to get through to the Nether Realm? How did you do it?"

"Nether Realm?" Lucy gasped. "Your case files never said anything about that."

"Liv worked with Jared. That night she, Jared and Jolie tried to open a portal to the Nether."

"Why didn't you tell me sooner?"

I shrugged in response. I didn't know what I could say placate her.

"Why would you do that?" Lucy turned to Jolie. "Everyone knows the Nether Realm is dangerous."

Jolie wrung her hands together. "I don't know. I just went along with what Jared said. I never knew why Liv wanted to get through. I never even knew about her involvement until the day it happened."

"Who or what came through that portal?" Lucy demanded. "Who else was there?"

Jolie shrugged. "I don't know. I just remember the portal opened. I got knocked out after that. When I woke up you were gone and Jared was dead."

"What about the other person? I know someone was in the cage next to me."

"I don't know. Just some girl Jared bought there."

"Wait, you never told me that. What girl?"

I demanded. "What did she look like?"

"I never got much of a look at her. Most of the night is a blur. I'm not sure I want to remember."

"Unbelievable!" Lucy stormed off.

I rushed after her. "Hey, where are you going?"

"I thought I could trust you. I thought you were on my side."

"I am."

"No, you're not. You proved you'd do anything to keep your family out of this. Or else you'd tell Ash. If your sister turned out to be the killer, you'd protect her too."

"That's —" I shut my mouth. I couldn't lie. Not about that.

Would I protect my sister? I'd do anything for her. But cover-up being a murderer? I couldn't answer that.

"Liv wouldn't kill anyone." Why did I have to keep telling people that? I knew my sister and I knew what she was capable of.

"Maybe she didn't have a choice. I got possessed by something. How do you know something didn't happen to her?"

"Because Liv was with us in the warehouse that night when the explosion went off. You were possessed; she wasn't."

"You can't be sure of that."

"Liv was with me the whole time. She didn't act any different than usual. When you were possessed you acted completely out of character."

"You're still not gonna tell Ash?"

"What good would that even do?"

"You're unbelievable." Lucy shook her head and stormed off.

I headed back into Jolie's room. "Give me your hand."

"What?" She furrowed her brow.

"Your hand. I wanna see if I can get a vision off you." I grabbed her hand. Closing my eyes, nothing came to me. *Stupid powers!*

"You don't see anything, do you?" Jolie tugged her hand from my grasp.

"Can you take us over to the other side?" I opened my eyes again.

"I already told you she's not there."

"The spirits tell you things, right? Maybe we can get more answers there."

Jolie shook her head. "I don't go there anymore."

"Why not?"

"Because the last time I did bad things appeared. I won't risk going back again." She shuddered. "Things are being scared out of the Nether — and that borders the spirit realm. It's better to stay out of it. Are you really trying to be a slayer again?"

"I don't think I have much choice in the matter."

"It's in our blood since Grandpa was a slayer too."

"Too bad I'm the only one who inherited the slayer genes."

Out of all of my grandparents' kids, only my birth mum became a slayer. Even Liv didn't have slayer abilities despite being the oldest.

"If we went into the spirit realm just this once, I'll be with you to help. Can you just — "

"No, Cassie. I'm not going back. I never meant for Liv to get hurt but I can't help you."

CHAPTER 21

ASH

Someone knocked on my door. I put down my beer and sighed. Being given the night off was rare for me. I wanted to kick back and relax. Cassie and I were meant to train today but she'd insisted on studying for her classes. Didn't she realise training was just as important? If not more so?

Groaning, I got up and headed over to my front door.

Lucy stood outside. "Good, you're in. We have a serious problem." She barged through the door when I opened it.

"What?"

"It's Cassie."

"Is she okay?" I pulled my phone out but didn't notice any messages from her or anyone else.

"No, she's out of her bloody mind. Her cousin was there the night of Jared's murder."

Now she had my attention. "Which cousin? She has a few."

"Jolie — she worked with Jared. She and Liv were there that night."

Jolie was involved? That surprised me.

"She doesn't plan on telling you. Ash, you need to talk some sense into her. She listens to you."

Sure she does. I almost laughed. "I'll try. What else d'you know?"

"Not much. She doesn't think telling you about Jolie is important."

"No doubt she wanted to protect her cousin."

"You'll take her in for questioning, right?"

"Lucy, the case has been closed. Officially at least."

"But you don't know who the killer is!" she protested.

"It's not my case. I fight monsters. Don't solve crimes as such. Cal is the official investigator." Cal wouldn't be happy if he found out we were still looking into the case.

Lucy stared at me, incredulous. "But Jolie knows things. And Cassie is too blind to see that. That's why you have to bring Jolie in."

"I can't tell Cal I'm looking into his case.

233

The queen declared the case closed. Elven politics are a more complicated than what you're used to doing human realm."

"So you're just gonna do nothing?" Lucy gaped me.

"I said I'd talk to her."

"There must be something more you can do."

"I'll try but getting a case reopened is hard. You need solid evidence. Even if Jolie is willing to make a statement it doesn't change anything. Not unless someone confesses."

"Great, then I carry on being treated like a murderer." Lucy slumped onto my sofa. "I thought coming to the academy would be a great opportunity."

"Elven society isn't perfect. But Cassie and I know you're innocent."

"Try telling that to everyone else."

"You don't want Jolie to suffer the same thing as you did, do you?"

Lucy opened and closed her mouth. "I want the guilty person to be punished. To know what really happened."

"I'll go talk to Cassie." I motioned for her to come with me. "Let's go."

To my surprise, Lucy came with me. I could have done without her there. But since she lived in the dorm I couldn't really object. I couldn't blame her for being angry either. Not after she had been sent to prison for a crime she didn't commit.

We headed up to the fifth floor of the housing block.

Lucy unlocked the door and Cassie frowned as we walked in.

"Seriously?" She rolled her eyes.

"Cass, we need to talk."

"No, we don't. I can't believe you went running to him after I told you —" She glowered at Lucy and gritted her teeth.

I stepped between them. "Why didn't you tell me about Jolie's involvement with Jared?"

"Because there's nothing to tell. She won't talk."

"'There must be more to it than that!" Lucy scoffed.

"Can you give us a minute alone?" I asked her.

Lucy sighed. "Fine." She stalked off but stopped around the corner out of sight.

"Let's go." I motioned to Cassie.

"No, you go. There's nothing else to talk about."

"Do you want a new magus?"

Her eyes widened. "Of course not."

"Well, I'm the only one you've got. And we

need to work together. For that we need complete trust between us."

"Trust takes time, Ash."

"Come on." I grabbed her arm and transported us out.

We reappeared at the entrance of the old lighthouse. Waves crashed around us and seagulls squawked overhead.

"What are you doing?" Cassie yanked her arm away from me.

"In case you didn't notice, Lucy was eavesdropping."

"I noticed." She scowled. "Why are we here?"

"So we can talk in private. What's Jolie's involvement?"

"You don't expect me to turn in my own cousin, do you?"

"I won't tell Cal. Not unless I have to."

"And you wonder why I won't trust you."

"Follow me." I headed down the spiral steps.

"Why?"

"Because I need to show you something."

We went down deep into the bowels of the lighthouse. The place most people didn't know existed. Crystal torches flickered on the walls and shadows danced around like watchful guardians.

"Is that a cell?" Cassie gasped when she spotted the bars and chains. "What the hell?"

"You remember I'm half light elf and half drow as well as part demon?" She nodded. "Well, every so often my demon side comes out. This is where I lock myself up. It's one of my biggest secrets." I knew her trusting me would take time but maybe this would help.

No one else knew about this place. Not even Rissa.

"Why, since when do you need to be locked up?" She furrowed her brow. "I thought you had your demon side under control? And you have that band." She motioned to my wrist.

"Every few months during a full moon I have to let my demon side out or it becomes…uncontrollable."

When we were kids, she'd been there for me after I had been bitten by a demon and imbued with its essence. I had been born half light elf, half dark elf. Turning into a part demon hadn't been part of the plan. The only good thing I got from it was my wings.

"I promise I won't tell Cal unless it is necessary."

"Enough people's lives have been ruined already." She sighed. "Jolie was involved with

Jared. He helped her push the limits of her abilities."

"Why didn't she come forward?"

"She was scared. Who could blame her."

"What were they doing?" There was the one thing no one had been able to work out.

Cassie took a deep breath. "Liv wanted to find someone in the Nether Realm. Don't ask me who or why because I have no idea."

"That's suicide. No one comes back from there." I rubbed my chin. "Wait, you didn't come to the academy to find a way through to the nether, did you?"

"I came to find out what happened to my sister. And... Because this is where I can learn how to control my powers."

"We need to figure out why she wanted to go there."

"Believe me, I'm trying." She bent and yanked up the heavy chains. "Isn't this a little extreme?"

"The demon has grown just as I have. My drow side doesn't help." I glanced at my watch. "It's late. You should go."

"Why?"

"Because I'll start changing." I shot into the cell and slammed the door shut.

"I've seen you change before."

"Would you please just go?" If she saw my

demon side she wouldn't want to stay. It wasn't the same as when we were kids. My demon side back then seemed like a hobgoblin compared to the beast I turned into now. I took off my watch and jacket and shoved them through the bars.

Cassie settled down on the floor by the door.

"You don't need to stay with me."

"Too bad. I'm staying." She crossed her arms. "I've seen you changed before so it's not a big deal."

Nothing I could say would make her leave. So I guessed I would have to put our friendship to the test and see if she really accepted me for what I was.

CHAPTER 22

CASSIE

My neck throbbed from where I'd fallen asleep outside the cell. I spent the night talking to Ash. He'd been right when he said his demon side had evolved. His skin turned the usual brow blue and his eyes went red. He'd growled and thrashed around a lot. Talking to him seemed to calm him down after a while.

I yawned as I opened the door to my dorm.

Murphy pounced on me the second I walked in. "Whoa!"

"Finally!" Lucy cried. "Where've you been? He's been driving us mad with his —"

"Incessant whining. Goddess, if you have sex with your boyfriend, can you get your dragon a babysitter first?" Ivy put her hands on her hips.

"Wait, what?" That woke me up. "I didn't have sex and Ash's not my boyfriend."

Murphy wrapped himself around me. Weird, I thought he'd be fine whilst I stayed with Ash most of the night.

"I need to get some work done." Ivy glared at me. "Please keep the noise down." She stalked off.

"Where were you?" Lucy asked. "Murphy drove us crazy."

"I'm sorry. I was... Busy."

"Something tells me you and Ash went talking about the case all night."

"You're too perky for someone who had no sleep."

"I stayed with Evie instead. So I got some sleep."

"We just talked." In truth, I'd done most of the talking.

"Is Jolie going to give a statement?"

"I can't force her to. Besides, what would it change?"

Lucy's shoulders slumped. "I guess you're right. I'm sorry I've been so bitchy."

"I —"

The walls shuddered as a loud explosion ripped through the air.

Now what?

"Ivy!" Lucy yelled.

We headed into her room which was filled with smoke.

"What the hell was that?"

"Minor setback." Ivy coughed from where she lay on the floor.

"Minor setback?" Lucy scoffed. "Are you trying to blow us up?"

"Maybe if I'd been able to get some sleep we wouldn't have this issue." Ivy shot me a glare.

I opened my mouth to speak when something smashed through the window.

Oh crap.

A blue skinned elf lunged at me.

Wonderful. It just had to be a drow.

"What the hell?" Lucy gasped.

"Go, get out of here." I waved my arm for them to leave.

Lucy and Ivy remained frozen.

"Go!" I spun and kicked the drow across the room.

"Is that real?" Lucy gasped.

The drow sprang up and hit me so hard I crashed into the wall.

"Yeah. Go to my room and get my sword. Hurry!" Murphy lunged at the drow, clawing at his eyes. The only way to kill a dark elf was stabbing them through the heart or to take off their head.

Drow weren't just dark elves — they were elves without souls. What elves became when they gave in to darkness.

Lucy ran off. I only hoped she'd do as I asked.

I glanced round the room for potential weapons.

Nothing.

Throwing a burst of light from my hand, the drow dodged it and my magic blew a hole in the wall.

"Cassie—" Ivy ducked out of the way as I forced the drow out of the room and into the hall.

I spun and kicked the drow to the ground.

I grabbed the kettle and bashed him over the head with it. It dented the kettle but didn't seem to deter him.

"Cassie!" Lucy threw my sword across the room.

It didn't get far. No surprise there given how heavy it was.

The drow knocked me down and punched me in the stomach.

I grunted and the air left my lungs in a whoosh.

Murphy clawed at the drow again then bit his hand. The drow swatted Murphy away.

"Cassie," Lucy yelled as the drow charged towards them.

Crawling across the floor, I reached for my sword. I grabbed it and leapt up. Dodging the drow's next blow I swung the sword at him.

Murphy bit down on the drow's fingers. The drow yelped and swatted my dragon away again.

"Hey, catch." Ivy pulled something out of her pocket and tossed it at the drow. It missed him.

Fire burst around us. The blast knocked me and Murphy across the room. I must have lost consciousness for a second.

My ears rang and everything around me became muffled.

"Murphy?" I croaked out.

Murphy came over and wrapped himself around my shoulders.

I coughed. It took a few seconds for the smoke to clear.

The walls of the dorm had been blown out. Now gaping holes stood in their place. Some of the outer wall had been blown out too.

Crap. What had Ivy done?

"Ow!" Someone groaned and scrambled out from under the debris.

Lucy.

At least my hearing had come back a bit.

"Are you okay?" I asked her.

She had a gash on her head and cuts across her arms.

"I guess. Where's Ivy? I can't believe she nearly killed us all!"

"I didn't plan on killing anyone." Ivy winced as she stumbled over. "Oh shit."

Oh shit seemed like the operative term. How the heck would we fix this?

"How can we explain this?" All colour drained from Ivy's face.

"Where's the drow?" Lucy asked.

"It's gone." I couldn't sense it anymore.

"I need to get out of here." Ivy turned to go.

Lucy grabbed her arm. "Whoa, hold your horses. You can't just blow up our dorm then run off."

"You don't understand. I'll be expelled. We all will. What was that thing?"

"It was a drow. An elf who has lost their soul." I spotted something glinting. I bent and grabbed my sword.

"Why do you even have a sword?" Ivy demanded. "What are you?"

"She's a slayer," Lucy remarked.

"A what? You mean like the elves talk about?" Ivy gaped at me.

"How do you know?" I asked Lucy.

"It's not hard to figure out. You're strong, you can fight. And your cousin is a McGregor. Plus, those runes on the sword say a slayer is the light in the shadows."

Lucy was much smarter than I'd expected. Most people didn't know how to read that form of old elvish that was written on my sword.

"What didn't you tell us?" Ivy demanded.

I shook my head. "It's supposed to be a secret. Why did you blow that drow up? I could —"

"Is anyone in here?" a voice called out.

I knew we'd be in deep shit for this.

After the enforcers had checked us over, Ivy, Lucy and I were brought to the chancellor's office.

Tree branches twisted around the back wall. The chancellor pinched the bridge of her nose. She sat behind a massive oak desk. On it was a shiny iMac and neatly stacked paperwork. "Do you have any idea what you three have done?" she demanded. "The entire floor was destroyed. Your room was decimated. What do you have to say for yourselves?"

We hadn't had time to discuss what we'd say. We all had minor cuts and bruises.

Luckily no one else had been on our floor. Everyone had left to go to the food court.

"A drow attacked us," I spoke up. "It broke through our window."

Ivy had been hellbent on running but couldn't after the enforcers showed up. She kept her eyes on the floor and Lucy's leg shook as she bit her lip.

The chancellor scoffed. "Why would a drow break into a fifth floor dorm room? And what in the nether caused the explosion?" she demanded. "Did you summon the drow?"

Ivy sank lower into her chair.

Lucy bit her lip harder. "Of course not. We were just talking about getting ready for breakfast. That thing came out of nowhere and attacked Cassie."

The chancellor's gaze shot over to me. "What kind of magic have you been practising, Miss Morgan? Did you go looking for the drow?"

I snorted. "No, I didn't."

"One of you must have done something. Drow don't just appear out of thin air," the chancellor snapped.

We all sat there in silence. I half expected one of to them speak up and tell her what I was. But they didn't.

"Who caused the explosion?" She scanned each of us. "Letting each of you come here was risky enough since you two have records." She motioned to Lucy and Ivy.

"I was pardoned," Lucy pointed out.

"And you" — she motioned to me — "Your sister is a —"

"My sister's not a killer." I gritted my teeth.

"I have no choice but to expel all of you given the substantial damage you caused to the housing block."

"No," Lucy gasped.

"You can't," Ivy protested.

I just sat there. My one chance of finding my sister had slipped away.

"I'm the one who caused the explosion," Ivy burst out. "That drow was gonna kill us. It was self-defence."

"What did you use?"

Ivy winced. "Some experimental magic."

The chancellor's jaw tightened. "I can't say I'm surprised given your record. I knew I should never have let you come to my academy."

My mind raced. I couldn't lose the chance to stay here. And I not only needed to find out answers about Liv, but this was the only place I could learn to control my powers.

"I'm a slayer — that's why the drow came."

The chancellor froze. "What?"

"You heard me. I'm a slayer. Estelle McGregor and Cal are my parents. So yes, I have pretty weird powers. I'm a slayer and given what's been happening here I'd say you're gonna need me around."

The chancellor pursed her lips together. "Then you're more dangerous than I ever imagined."

I crossed my arms. "You and the enforcers can't fight what's coming out of the nether on your own. Like it or not, you need me. A slayer with unpredictable powers is better than no slayer at all."

She snorted. "We don't need you."

I arched an eyebrow. "Really? Are you gonna tell everyone about the creatures that keep coming out of the nether then?"

If she did that, there'd be mass panic. Dozens of students would leave and it risked the academy being closed down. People depended on this island for their livelihoods and the illusion of safety the enforcers provided — I doubted the chancellor would risk that.

"Let us stay. I'll take care of the drow and anything else that comes through."

"Why? You're all reckless. A murderer, a slayer and a pyromaniac." Her lip curled. "I can't allow any of you to stay on my island."

"It's not your island," Lucy pointed out. "I doubt the queen'd be happy finding out you had the chance to stop things from getting out of control."

"Let us stay. Please." Ivy gripped the edge of the table. "I can't lose my place here and I was just protecting them."

The chancellor slammed her hands down on her desk. "My decision is final. Collect your belongings and leave at once. I want you off this island."

This is so unfair! Power pulsed from my hands.

The chancellor froze in place.

"Not again." I groaned.

"Did you do that?" Lucy gasped.

Ivy put her head in her hands. "Now we'll be in even more trouble."

"I can't help it! It's not like I can control it." I sighed. "We should go."

"I can't believe you're just giving up." Lucy gaped at me.

"She's right. We can't leave," Ivy agreed.

Wow, they'd finally agreed on something.

"I don't want to leave either but I don't know what else to do to convince her."

"What about your dad?" Ivy asked. "Maybe he could do something."

"He's not my dad. He's… Nothing to me." I didn't want to call Cal. Somehow I doubted he would help anyway.

"But he can help," Lucy said. "I know you hate him, but he could talk to her."

"I doubt it. This just proves I'm dangerous to have on the island."

"Bollocks. We are staying on this island." Ivy rummaged around in her back. "I have a glamour powder."

Lucy grinned, "Good idea. Cassie, you're a light elemental. You can create glamour."

I stared at them in disbelief. "Haven't you seen how unpredictable my magic has been?"

"Yeah, but you're strong too. Hold out your hands and visualise what you want to create."

"Hurry," Ivy said and threw dust in my face.

I sneezed as the dust tickled against my skin.

Lucy and Ivy ducked outside the door.

"Focus on what Cal looks like," Ivy hissed.

The chancellor unfroze and stood up. Dust tingled over my skin.

"Chancellor," I said in Cal's deep voice.

"How — how did —" She gaped at me.

Goddess, was it working?

"My daughter and her friends are to stay here on the island, are we clear?"

"But —"

I growled at her. "You can be assured Cassie won't be a problem. Have a new dorm room assigned to her and her friends. And if you breathe one word about Cassie being the slayer to anyone, I'll have you off this island and out of Elfhame."

I stormed out and prayed my little magic trick had worked.

CHAPTER 23

CASSIE

"That was close," I breathed as I headed off down the hall with the others.

"Too close," Lucy agreed. "Do you think it worked?"

"If it hadn't, she would've already thrown us off the island," I remarked. "Why didn't you two out me?"

"Because I'm your friend, obviously." Lucy rolled her eyes. "You're the only one I've got on this island."

"I'm your friend too." Ivy gave a faint smile.

"We all need to be extra careful," I added. "Or they'll find an excuse to get rid of us. We better get to class. Or there won't be any time left for breakfast."

"What about housing? We don't have a dorm anymore," Lucy pointed out.

"We'll find out about a dorm later. Maybe we could shower at Ash's."

"We don't have time for that." Lucy took hold of our arms. "We need to use some hocus-pocus. Repeat after me, *'pota prope.'*"

Ivy and I repeated the words. The dust and grime on us faded.

"What was that?" Ivy frowned.

"Elvish and fae words for clean. Not as nice as a shower but just as effective."

"Now let's get some breakfast."

We all hurried down to the food court. If we grabbed something quick, we would just have time for some breakfast before classes began for the day.

People sent curious glances our way. No doubt gossip would spread about what happened on our floor.

Mike came over and joined us. "Hey, what the hell happened? Everyone's saying you three blew up your dorm."

Ivy snorted. "It wasn't intentional."

"It's a long story." Murphy growled as he flew back over onto my shoulder.

Why did he keep doing that?

"We need a new room," Lucy added. "But the housing office said they don't have any left. What if we can't find a new dorm?"

"My aunt owns the nightclub here on the island. She could probably give us room."

"We need three rooms," Ivy said. "I'm not sharing a room with that dragon. He'll steal my stuff!"

"You're not going to be keeping explosives in our next dorm room." Lucy glared at her.

"So what happened?" Mike prompted.

We all glanced at each other, unsure what to say.

I couldn't tell Mike what I was. Not because I didn't trust him but because enough people knew already.

"We were attacked by something and Ivy's magic goo took out the entire floor," Lucy explained.

Mike's jaw dropped. "Attacked by what?"

I shrugged. "Some weird blue skinned guy."

"There's lots of strange things coming out of the nether," Ivy agreed.

The rest of breakfast passed with more awkward questions.

I was almost relieved when we headed for our first class for the day. Spell casting. I'd picked out a new class as I had found some of the others boring. My tests had shown I had strong spellcasting abilities. Other than saying the odd rhyme here and there I'd never excelled at formal spellcasting.

Lucy and Ivy had the class with me. Then I had training with Ash later.

Lucy and Ivy seemed more excited about the class and I was. I hoped this class wouldn't turn into a complete disaster. I'd already endured one this morning and I could do without another one.

"Welcome to the class, I'm Ava Norbury. Today we're going to be going over the fundamentals of spellcasting."

Much to my dismay, Elora was in the class too. Why did the perfect elven princess want to learn spells? Didn't she have someone to do that for her?

"Oh look, the pyromaniacs are here." Elora sneered when she spotted us.

Ivy vanished from view. I envied her ability to go invisible.

"Have you moved on from stabbing people?" someone asked Lucy.

Ava started rambling on about different magic systems and how her classes took elements from fae, elven and witch systems.

Maybe that would work better for me.

"Now we're going to perform a test to see what each of you have in terms of abilities. That way we can make sure you're getting the right lessons. Some people will be good at basic ritual or high spellcasting." Ava waved her hand and crystals appeared on the table in front of us. "Place your hands on the crystal."

Oh crap. This was the last thing I needed given what had happened when I had first come to the academy.

"Just relax. You'll be fine," Lucy whispered.

Easy for you to say. You've you're not the one with the freaky magic.

Something landed with a thump beside my feet.

"Holy crap, Murphy. You're not supposed to be here," I hissed. "Get in here." I motioned to my bag. Murphy ignored me and sniffed around other people's bags. "Murphy!" I bent to grab him but he scooted out of my way.

"Just let him wander," Lucy said. "He's curious."

"He's a pain," I wanted to say but didn't.

We all placed our hands on the crystals. A rainbow of light filled the classroom.

I pulled my hands away as light whirled around my crystal. Glancing under the table I couldn't see any sign of Murphy.

Great. Just great.

My senses recoiled from the energy.

Ava came over to me, mouth agape. "What did you do?"

"I didn't do anything."

"Her magic is very... Unpredictable," Ivy remarked.

Ava grabbed my arm. Energy jolted through me and my eyes snapped shut.

Ava stood talking to my gran and... My birth mum...

Ava drew away from me and all colour drained from her face.

Holy —

Energy pulsed around the room and froze everyone except Ava.

Not again.

"Are... Are you like Estelle?" Ava put her hand to her chest.

"I'm...her daughter. You knew my mum?"

"Many years ago." She nodded. "Did you join my class to question me about her?"

"No, why?"

"Your sister came to see me a few months ago. Asked a lot of questions about your mother."

"What —"

My magic wore off and noise filtered back through the room again.

"Okay, class. I'll split you into groups and give you each an assignment." Ava turned away from me.

And I wondered why Liv would ask her anything.

Once class was over, Ava left before I had the chance to question her again. Meanwhile my mind was reeling. Why would Liv ask her anything?

Liv never even talked about our birth mum. To me, she just pretended like a still never even existed. After a while I just learnt to accept it. Mum didn't like talking about her sister either.

Too bad I didn't remember much about my life with her.

That didn't mean I wasn't curious about it.

I still didn't understand why no one had files on Estelle's death.

Wouldn't the death of the last slayer have been big news. Estelle have been pretty infamous — I did remember that much.

The rest of the day passed in a blur of classes. And more training with Ash.

Lucy and Ivy came to find me after I finished training and I went to the food court to have dinner with them.

"Any news on our new dorm?" Ivy wanted to know.

"Someone sent me a message whilst you were in training." Lucy pulled out her phone. "Shit!"

"What?" Ivy demanded. "Did they say no to our new dorm? Do have to share a room? Because that wouldn't work for me."

"They gave us rooms but it's on the other side of the island." Lucy held up her phone. "It says our new dorm is in the north tower. It's not even on this academy map."

"North Tower?" I frowned at the message. "Where is that?"

I furrowed my brow as I read the message. "Why would they house us all the way out there?"

"In case anything attacks again." Ivy scowled.

"Let's go and check it out before we jump to conclusions."

We headed out to where the north tower stood. It looked over us all imposing grey, weathered stone and filthy windows that looked like soulless eyes. It didn't look very inviting.

"This place was once used by the enforcers but hasn't been used for anything in the last decade or so," Lucy explained. " I remember reading something about it when I first came here."

"How do know all this stuff?" Ivy wanted to know.

"Because I actually read all of the welcome book. And all the history I could find on the island and the academy."

"This place is a dump."

We had to go to the housing office to get keys to the tower. They hung on a big metal ring. It took a few tries before I finally pried the door open. We all coughed as a wave of dust flew out.

"They can't expect us to live here, can they?" Ivy covered her mouth with her shirt.

The windows were so filthy they only let faint cracks of light in.

Lucy shuddered. "This place needs a deep clean before anyone could live here."

"At least it has a roof," I said, thinking about our broken dorm room.

"It's disgusting." Lucy grimaced.

"Well, we'll just have to make do, I guess. The housing office said all the other rooms are full up."

"You said your sister's apartment was free," Lucy remarked.

"Yeah, but it's only got one bedroom and not much other space. It's not big enough for all of us."

We went around opening windows as we went.

The kitchen looked worse. I turned the tap on and brown water came out.

Next, we headed upstairs. To my surprise, there were three rooms and a larger room on the top floor.

It might not be perfect but for now it was home.

CHAPTER 24

CASSIE

Lucy and I headed out to the island's nightclub, Nocturne, that night. I couldn't remember the last time I'd been to a club. Usually when I went to one I was working a case. Mum and I took suspected infidelity cases sometimes. Not my fave kind of case but usually good money.

Coloured light flashed overhead and music pulsed with heavy vibrations. Good thing I'd left Murphy at the tower. He'd hate a place like this. The club had red coloured walls and a dark shiny dance floor that flashed with light.

I wore jeans and a sparkly vest top. Lucy had on a short black mini dress and black wedges. Ivy hadn't wanted to come with us.

Probably for the best since the club wasn't her scene.

"Your aunt actually owns this place?" Lucy said over the roaring music. "How did that happen?"

I shrugged. "Guess she saw an opportunity here."

I headed over to the bar and waved to my aunt, Jenna.

"Cassie!" She grinned and leaned over the bar to hug me.

"Hi, Auntie." I returned her hug. "Good to see you."

"Never thought I'd see you come to school here. Bet Nina is freaking out, isn't she?"

"Oh yeah. She's not happy. Auntie, was anyone here good friends with Liv?"

My aunt's smile faded and she sighed. "Cass, Nina already interviewed everyone here."

"Think. Someone here must know something."

"You're welcome to question people but I doubt you'll find any answers." She turned away. "I have to get back to work."

I started off by talking to some of the barmaids. Neither of the women said much. Other than Liv seemed cool but kept to herself most of the time. I considered talking to Jolie again but doubted she tell me anything new. The rest of the night passed in a blur as I tried asking other people questions about my sister — which led nowhere. Lucy dragged me over to the bar at one point and insisted I had a drink or two.

I turned back to my aunt when she was closing up later that night.

Lucy had fallen asleep in one of the booths.

"Auntie, come on, you must know something."

"Cass, don't you think I'd tell you if I did? My advice would be let it go."

"Now you sound like my mum. Why are you all so eager to give up on finding Liv?"

"Because she tried to get to the nether. Nothing good comes from that."

"That doesn't mean she's dead," I protested.

"If she were alive, don't you think she would have contacted you by now?"

My heart sank. She had a point. Liv and I rarely went long without talking to each other.

"Liv wasn't even showing up for work very often," my aunt said. "She was too caught up in that mess with that necromancer."

"She wasn't?" I frowned.

That didn't sound like my sister.

Time to talk to my cousin again.

After telling Lucy to go home, I headed up to the housing block.

"When did you and Jared use to work?" I said when Jolie opened the door.

"It's the middle of the night." She yawned. "Can't this wait?"

"No, answer the question."

Jolie's eyelids drooped. "Work?"

I shook her shoulders to wake her up. "Jo, my sister is missing because you messed around with dangerous magic. So please tell me what you know!" Maybe those drinks hadn't been such a good idea now. All that did was fuel my anger even more.

"We worked at my shop in Colchester. But you won't find anything there as it's been let to someone else."

I sighed. "Think. Where did you and Jared train when he was teaching you about your powers?"

"At my shop and... at his house. You know... where it happened."

"The place wasn't even lived in. He just used it as a cover. Where else did you meet with him?"

"Those are the only places. And the old warehouse."

I knew there was nothing to find at the warehouse.

After a few more questions, I still didn't get any useful answers.

Maybe the answers weren't with Jolie but somewhere with Liv.

Since the next day was Saturday I texted Ash and told him I had to miss training that morning.

I had to go through Liv's things and look for potential clues. The tower had turned out better than I expected. Having a larger room for me and Murphy had come in handy.

Lucy had rustled up some more mismatched furniture from somewhere. So I had a bed, a desk, chest of drawers and a wardrobe. I'd painted the walls white for now as they looked better than the stark grey stone.

One by one I went through the boxes of Liv's stuff and laid it all out. Most of it was clothes, jewellery, books and other knickknacks. Along with several photos. Nothing mentioned Jared or the Nether Realm.

A loud knock came at the door.

Ash, my senses told me.

Groaning, I headed over and opened the door. "What are you doing here?"

"Might ask you the same thing. You can't keep missing training."

"A couple of days won't hurt."

"Your powers are still unpredictable. You need to train as much as possible." Ash glanced around the room. "You're still working on the case."

"You don't expect me to give up, do you? Because I won't."

"I know that but you need to —"

"I'm not losing control of my powers as often and nothing's attacked me for a while. Maybe we can ease back on the training a bit."

"Have you found anything new?" Ash shut the door behind him and tossed his leather jacket onto the chair.

"Nothing." I sighed. "I've been up all night and haven't found a thing. I still don't know why Liv would want to find anyone in the Nether Realm. She's never lost anyone apart from our mum."

"Maybe that's the answer."

"What?"

"You both lost Estelle."

"Yeah, but she's dead."

"No one really knows what happened that night."

"Someone might."

"Who?"

"Cal."

"Goddess, you can't expect me to talk to him."

"He was her magus. He knew her better than anyone."

I looked away. "You know how I feel about him."

"I do, but what do you have to lose? He was there for you."

I snorted. "When?" I couldn't believe he'd suggested such a thing.

"He used to visit you every weekend when we were kids."

"That doesn't make him my father. No, I'm not talking to him. Not yet." I leaned back against my bed. "If Liv planned this, why is there no proof? My sister was always meticulous when she planned anything."

"Maybe she hid her plans."

"Jared must've had a base somewhere. Do you have any more files in him?"

"Not any that I haven't already given you." Ash leaned back in the chair. "Who would your sister confide in? Other than you?"

I shrugged. "Other than Mum…no one. I told you, she didn't trust many people."

"There must be someone. We all have someone we trust more than anyone."

"Oh, yeah? Who do you trust?" I arched an eyebrow at him.

"You probably. Even Tye doesn't know what I am."

I smiled. It felt good to have some trust back between us. Almost like we were kids again. "Aside from her ex-girlfriend, who I've already talked to, I can't think of anyone."

"Not even Nina?"

I scoffed. "If she knew what Liv had planned, she would have shut it down faster than we could blink."

"People tend to confide in family and close friends. What about your cousins?"

I shook my head. "We didn't see them much after Estelle died. Other than Jolie and Jada. Jada knows what happened but she didn't see Liv again until just before she vanished."

"What about your gran?"

I laughed. "That's doubtful. Mum kept us away from her after Estelle's death. They argued a lot. But…" I trailed off.

Grandma hadn't been surprised about Liv or when I'd been summoned before the Elven Council. Did she know something?

My phone paused and signalled I had a message. Finally, a message from my sister's bank. To my surprise Liv had some pretty strong security in place around her financials. Nothing I'd tried had allowed me access and I had to formally make a request to the bank to get any details.

"Liv's bank sent me her statement." I swore under my breath when I caught sight of all the money in there. "Where did all of this come from?"

Ash glanced over my shoulder and whistled. "That's a lot of money. But that's not surprising. Her music did really well back in the day."

I skimmed through the different recent transactions. No money had left her account since she had disappeared. My stomach dropped when I saw that. But one name stood out to me. Magda McGregor. She'd been sending my sister money.

Why would Liv need money from her? Only one way to find out.

"Let's go," Ash said.

"What?"

"To see your gran, I mean."

I gaped at him. "How —"

"I know how your mind works. So let's go."

Ash and I reappeared in my gran's sitting room. Pictures of different family members hung across the ivory walls and a fur rug covered the plush pink carpet.

"I wondered when you'd come to see me." Grandma looked up from where she sat by the ornate stone fireplace.

"Would do you know about Liv's disappearance? Why were you sending her money?" I asked.

"It was it was her own money. I put every penny she made from her music career into a trust for her."

"Do you know why she wanted to go to the Nether Realm?" Ash asked.

Grandma's icy gaze fixed on him. "You're lucky I'm letting you into my house, magus. But I can't say I am surprised you're here. You always were devoted to Cassie."

"Grandma, answer our questions," I snapped.

She blew out a breath. "Olivia came to me a few months ago. Asked me lots of questions about Estelle. About how she died. She kept having nightmares about the night those drow attacked your house."

Liv had been seventeen when Estelle died. About a year into her music career. She hadn't been around much as she'd always been travelling. Nina had gone with her since Estelle always insisted she couldn't leave. Her duties as a slayer were too important.

"Wait, Liv was there when Estelle was killed? Why did you never tell me that?" I demanded.

"That's right. She came home for a visit. I forgot about that," Ash mused.

"Grandma, why can't I remember that night? A seer said my memories are cloaked."

"Because I used my magic to make you forget those awful events. No child should have to remember the horrors of what happened."

"You erased Liv's memories too." I froze.

Grandma nodded. "That's why she came to me. Said she'd been working with that Jared. Somehow that triggered her memories. She said someone else was there that night. A woman who attacked Estelle."

"Who?"

Grandma shook her head. "I don't know. I never found out. As the years went by it didn't matter so much. I've lost enough people already. I know you want justice but do not walk down thar path. It will only lead to death."

"But Liv's not —"

Grandma reached out and squeezed my hand. "Olivia is gone, Cassie. It's hard for all of us to admit. Following in her footsteps won't lead to anything good."

CHAPTER 25

CASSIE

The next few weeks passed in a blur of classes and more training. I still refuse to believe my sister was dead. My family might have given up on her but I never would. Ash seemed to convinced the key to the whole case lay with Jared but I wasn't so sure. I spent hours going through Liv's stuff but found nothing.

After my history class, I went back to my room to study for a while. I slumped onto my bed and pulled out my laptop and books. A meowing sound made me look up.

Murphy flew off in excitement. He loved having a playmate.

"Did Ivy forget to feed her cat?" I followed after him.

Salem scratched at the door of Ivy's room which she had closed.

I knew her stay-out-of-my-room rule but heck, I was only letting her cat in. Turning the handle, both Salem and Murphy bounced inside. "Murph, you know Ivy doesn't want you in here." I hurried in after him.

Murphy and Salem chased each other around the room. The cat jumped onto Ivy's desk and sent files flying. Murphy followed suit. Both cat and dragon seemed determined to outdo each other.

"Murphy, out. You're messing everything up." I bent and picked up a file. Pieces of paper fell out. They were newspaper clippings about Jared's murder and Lucy's arrest. Along with reports of the warehouse explosion. Weird, why would she have these? She didn't strike me as a true crime type. Ivy had never shown any interest in the case so I couldn't imagine why she had these.

I put the files back and picked up a diary that had fallen open. It was booked marked with the date Liv went missing. The words "meeting with J" struck me. Along with a list of different chemicals.

"What are you doing in my room?" Ivy demanded as she came in.

"You're the other victim, aren't you?" I stared at her, dumbfounded.

Ivy's mouth fell open. "No! I mean, I told you to stay out!" She yanked the diary from my hands. "Get out!"

"It was you. You're good at making yourself invisible and you know how to blow up a warehouse."

Ivy grabbed a knife from her desk.

Murphy shot towards her and grabbed the blade.

Tears streamed down her face. "Please, I never meant for this to happen. I didn't kill Jared. I needed his help. I just wanted to see my parents again."

"Then who killed Jared?"

"The shadows. One of them went into Lucy. Lucy fought against him. That's how she got burned. But someone else appeared. She killed him."

"Who?"

She shook her head. "I don't know. I didn't see them clearly but I think it was a woman."

"You need to come with me to Cal and tell the truth."

"What? No? They'd lock me up."

"Not if you tell the truth this time. Ivy, this won't go away."

She backed away from me. "I can't."

"You have to do. What would your parents what you do?"

"Doesn't matter. It's my fault they're gone. If I hadn't —" She cried harder.

Ash, can you come over? I found the other victim. It's Ivy. I reached out to him with my mind.

What? I'm on my way. Ash appeared in a flash of light. "Ivy, I'm here to take you to the enforcers tower."

I gave Ash a quick rundown on what I had found then headed out of the room.

"Ivy, what happened to my sister?" I demanded. "You had to be in that warehouse to trigger the explosion."

"No, I didn't. I — I followed Lucy. When you and your sister came I panicked and… I never meant for anyone to get hurt. I don't even know why the explosion went off."

"Was there someone else in the warehouse with you?"

"I don't know. I heard your sister talking to someone but I didn't see anything. I got scared and ran out of there. Then the explosion went off."

"Ash, can taking her in wait a few minutes?"

He crossed his arms. "It better not be long."

"Lily?" I called out as I headed out of the room. "Lily, I need you."

Lily appeared in a whirl of smoke. "What now?"

"I found out who was with Lucy on the night of the murder."

She beamed. "Good, want me to take their soul?"

"No! I need you to bring the spirits of her parents here."

Lily gaped at me. "What? I'm not your personal reaper, slayer. There are —"

"Look, me and my sister helped you when you wanted to find Lucy. Now, I need you to return the favour. Bring Ivy's parents here. Just let her say a proper goodbye to them." Lily vanished. I headed back to Ivy's room where she was still sobbing and Ash sorted through the evidence.

Lily reappeared a few moments later. "We'd better be even after this, slayer."

A man and a woman appeared. The man was tall with floppy dark hair and blue eyes. The woman petite and redhaired like Ivy.

Ivy sniffed. "Mum? Dad?"

"We're even," I told Lily.

"Ivy?" The woman held her arms out and Ivy rushed into them.

"Mum, I'm so sorry. I never meant for you —" Ivy sobbed against her mother's shoulder.

"Ivy, you're not responsible for your parents' deaths. It was their time," Lily said and leaned back against the wall.

"Of course you weren't." Ivy's dad hugged her. "Sometimes bad things happen but we're always watching over you. We love you so much."

"Ivy, you know you have to do the right thing," her mum told her. "Tell the Elhanan the truth."

Ivy sniffed then nodded. She clung to her parents awhile longer.

Ash and I took Ivy to the enforcers tower. Cal and the other enforcers questioned her length. When Jolie heard the news she decided she wanted to tell her story as well.

Lucy hadn't been happy when she heard about Ivy's revelation but Lucy let her come back to the tower after some convincing. She was still our friend no matter what she done and she had been caught up in the mess just like Lucy had.

Despite the recent revelations, I still had no clue what had happened to my sister.

CHAPTER 26

ASH

I headed out to the north tower around noon the next day. I hadn't seen much of Cassie or her friends over the past few days. The recent revelation about Ivy had shocked us all. But Cassie and Lucy seemed determined to stand by their friend. Now the term was ending and we'd be leaving the island soon for the summer. I'd wanted to close the case and get Cassie's some answers before then so I had spent the last few days doing as much research as I could.

Cassie and I hadn't been training as much but at least her powers were controllable more. She'd made good progress over the last few weeks since first coming to the academy.

"Hey, I think I found a way of figuring out what happened to your sister," I told Cassie as I headed into her kitchen.

"Hello to you too," Lucy grumbled.

"Oh. Right. Hi."

"How?" Cassie asked. "Nothing we've tried so far has helped." She sipped her coffee.

"It's a pretty advanced spell that you and I can cast."

"What kind of spell?"

"An elven spell. Found it in one of the old grimoires. It's like a vision quest. It helps you to find whatever you're seeking."

"Vision quest can be dangerous," Lucy remarked. "Any number of things can go wrong."

"I'll be right there with you and could pull you out of anything went wrong," I added.

Cassie frowned. "Since when are you so eager to do something dangerous?"

"Since... You need help."

"And?"

"Look, you'll never got full control of your powers if you don't get a handle your emotions. For that you need to know what happened to your sister."

"Can I see the spell?" Lucy asked. Lucy seemed to know a lot more about spells than most of the teachers on the island.

I handed her the parchment.

"What happens in this quest?" Cassie prompted. "How does it work?"

"You experience whatever you're searching for." Lucy's eyes roamed over the page. "Says here it helps if you have something that belongs to the victim."

Murphy flew over onto the table and dropped a heart-shaped pendant in front of Cassie.

"Where'd you get that?" Cassie gasped. "Vinessa had it. Liv traded it to her."

"I wouldn't recommend stealing things from that woman," I remarked. "Maybe you should get him to take it back."

"I didn't steal it. Murphy's sneaks things away from people all the time."

"You shouldn't be surprised by his sneakiness," Lucy said. "Are you sure this spell isn't too risky? What if you get stuck?"

"I'll be there," I pointed out.

"You've only been a magus again a few weeks," Lucy said. "Maybe you should ask —"

"We're not asking Cal anything. He'd never agreed to this." Cassie scowled.

"Maybe we should talk to him," I agreed.

Cassie gaped at me. "What? Why?"

"Not about the spell, about your mum. Maybe he'd know something. I'll go with you, if you want."

"Fine. But he won't know anything."

Cassie and I headed out to Cal's apartment. He had a penthouse in a private housing block. She didn't say anything on the way over.

Cal opened the door and his eyes widened when he caught sight of his daughter.

"What happened to my mum the night she died?" Cassie demanded.

"I'll go and get some tea or —" I said.

"I don't want tea, Ash. I want answers." She threw me a glare.

Okay.

Cal sighed and sank into the leather armchair. "Your sister came and asked me the same thing a few months ago."

Cassie narrowed her eyes. "Why didn't you tell me that before now?"

I wanted to know that too. Cal had to know we were still looking into Liv's disappearance.

"I told Nina and she was livid."

"Why would Liv come to see you of all people?" Cassie asked. "She hated you."

"Because I was there the night Estelle was killed. Your sister came and asked me what I knew."

"What did you tell her?"

"By the time I got there it was too late." Cal looked away. "Estelle was dead and you were unconscious. Olivia asked me about who attacked your house. Told her I couldn't be sure. The drow that I tracked down claimed that someone led them there."

"Who?"

"I don't know the name that your mother mentioned an elven witch. Said she was having issues with her. I never found anything about the witch," Cal admitted. "Your sister asked a lot of questions about her."

"Why didn't you tell me any of this?" Cassie repeated.

"Would you have listened?" Cal arched a brow.

"You should have told me. What else did you tell Liv?"

"There's nothing to tell. I was too late. I lost your mother that night. I lost everything including you. I know you hate me but I never meant to lose her. I loved her more than anything."

"If you know what Liv was doing, why didn't you do anything to stop her?" Cassie demanded.

"I did. I called Nina, who said she'd handle it."

Cassie got up and stormed out.

I made a move to go after her.

"Don't," Cal said.

"Don't what?"

"Don't fall in love with her. You have seen what a mess a slayer and magus falling in love causes. I see how close you two are getting."

"I'm not falling for her," I snapped. "Even if I was, I'm not you."

I hurried outside and found Cassie crying and on the steps. "Hey." I put an arm around her. "It's okay."

"Why does everyone keep hiding things from me? I am sick of it!"

"Maybe we should talk to Nina."

She shook her head. "I don't need to. I know why she didn't tell me. She didn't want me doing the same thing as Liv. That's why she wants me to stop searching for her." She buried her head against my shoulder. "Thanks."

"For what?"

"For being here."

I hugged her back. "I'll always be there for you."

"I want to do the spell."

"Are you sure?"

She nodded. "I know there's risk, but I need to know what happened to Liv."

A pit of dread knotted in my stomach.

Lucy was right. I hadn't become magus. Instead of learning spellcasting, I'd become a warrior. But I had the power to help her do this and I'd do it.

One way or another we'd find out what happened to her sister.

Cassie and I sat in the circle surrounded by candles later that night in one of the rooms in the lighthouse. "Are you sure you want to do this?" I asked. Nerves had been getting the better of me all day.

She nodded. "This was your idea and you seemed pretty gung-ho about it."

"If something goes wrong —"

"It won't. I trust you."

I smiled. "Good. Let's get started." I took hold of her hands.

Together we chanted the spell.

Light blazed around us and the circle faded. I found myself outside on the street with Cassie — in Colchester.

Why were we here?

Liv walked past us, glancing around, uneasy.

"Liv." Cassie gasped. She didn't pay attention to us and I had to remind myself this wasn't real.

Liv carried on walking and headed into the warehouse where Jared waited. Jolie lay slumped on the ground.

Liv paled when she caught sight of her cousin. "What's wrong with her?"

"We need her to get through to the nether. Don't worry about her. She's just taking a little nap. You're not having second thoughts, are you?" Jared reached out to touch her face but Liv brushed him off.

"No. I will find out who killed my mother," Liv snapped. "How close are we to opening the portal?"

"A couple of hours, maybe. Once that kid Ivy brings us the book we'll have that portal open."

She knew about Ivy! Cassie paled.

Liv wrung her hands together. "Good. I don't want anyone else to get hurt, okay?"

"Of course not, my sweet." Jared pulled her in for a kiss and she flinched.

Geez, Liv, what are you doing? Cassie remarked.

Why did finding Estelle's killer matter so much? Was it because she remembered something? Liv and Estelle never got along. They'd always argued. So I didn't buy the idea that this was about revenge. And I doubted Cassie did either.

The scene changed and we found ourselves in the warehouse only this time Cassie, Liv and Lucy were there.

Holy crap, why am I seeing myself? Cassie gasped.

"We're taking you into custody," Past Cassie told Lucy and pulled out her cuffs.

"No, you don't understand —" Lucy protested.

Liv raised her hand light exploded around us. It knocked Past Cassie and Lucy to the ground.

Whoa, Liv had been the one who knocked us unconscious? That doesn't make sense. I'd been so sure it had been the explosion, Cassie told me.

I couldn't say I was surprised. I'd suspected Liv might have been more involved but I knew Cassie would never accept it. Not unless she saw proof.

"Sorry, sis." Liv pulled out a piece of parchment. "I really am sorry. I never wanted anyone to get hurt." She chanted a spell in old elvish.

Light flashed and fizzled out.

"Argh, why didn't it work?" Liv gritted her teeth, then reached down and grabbed Past Cassie's hand. A portal formed and a woman stepped out of it.

"You again," the woman growled. "Why do you keep summoning me?"

Liv grabbed the woman by the throat and slammed her against the wall. "Because killed my mother. But someone sent you, didn't they?"

My mouth fell open. Liv had slayer strength. No, that wasn't possible. Estelle tested her all the time. Liv never showed any signs of slayer powers.

"I'm just a messenger," the woman said. "I was ordered to kill your mother…"

"By whom?"

"The Queen of the Nether. She needed a slayer to open the portal to this world." The woman threw a blast of light at her.

Liv screamed as light struck her in the stomach. Liv blasted the woman with a burst of energy and the woman screamed as her body exploded. Liv turned back to the glowing portal. Tendrils of purple wild magic streamed out. She made a step through then screamed as her body exploded in a burst of light.

I gasped as the warehouse around us faded. I caught hold of Cassie as she fell forward.

"She's gone. My sister's gone." She buried her head against her shoulder.

EPILOGUE

CASSIE

As the end of term finally came around, I still didn't know how to deal with the revelation about my sister's death. So much had changed in the last few months since I had joined the academy and learnt how to be a slayer again. I almost felt relieved at the chance of going home for the summer. And of seeing my mum again.

When I headed home, she wrapped her arms around me and let me cry. She started crying too, and I knew it was a relief for both of us to let out some of our repressed grief.

Together with my family and friends we had a ceremony to finally lay Liv to rest. We might not have a body but that didn't mean we couldn't say goodbye to her. The ritual took place at Grandma's house and she led it, saying prayers for Liv.

Ash came up behind me afterwards and hugged me. "You'll be okay," he told me.

I sniffed. "How'd you know that?"

"Because I know you. You're the strongest person I know. Are you gonna come back to the academy next term?"

Going back to the academy hadn't been part of my plan originally. I had only gone there to get my powers under control. I didn't have complete control yet but that would come with time. Heck, I hadn't even planned on staying for the full term — Only until I had found out what happened to my sister. Now I knew that... I didn't know what to do. I never expected to find friends and find a place on the island.

"I'll go back," I said after a while. "I'm still the slayer and I'm not going to walk away when there's still work to be done. Someone killed Estelle — that's what led to Liv's death. And I'll damn well find out who they are."

CONTINUED IN BOOK 2

If you enjoyed this book it would be great if you could leave a review. For more news about my books sign up for my newsletter on tiffanyshand.com/newsletter

ALSO BY TIFFANY SHAND

ELFHAME ACADEMY SERIES

Elfhame Academy Prequel Collection

Elfhame Academy Book 1

EXCALIBAR INVESTIGATIONS SERIES

Touched by Darkness Book 1

Bound to Darkness Book 2

Rising Darkness Book 3

Excalibar Investigations Complete Box Set

SHADOW WALKER SERIES

Shadow Walker

Shadow Spy

Shadow Guardian

Shadow Walker Complete Box Set

ANDOVIA CHRONICLES

Dark Deeds Prequel

The Calling

The Rising

Hidden Darkness

Morrigan's Heirs

ROGUES OF MAGIC SERIES

Bound By Blood

Archdruid

Bound By Fire

Old Magic

Dark Deception

Sins Of The Past

Reign Of Darkness

Rogues Of Magic Complete Box Set Books 1-7

ROGUES OF MAGIC NOVELLAS

Wyvern's Curse

Forsaken

On Dangerous Tides

The Rogues of Magic Short Story Collection

EVERLIGHT ACADEMY TRILOGY

Everlight Academy, Book 1: Faeling

Everlight Academy Book 2: Fae Born

Everlight Academy Book 3: Fae Light

Everlight Tales Short Story Collection

THE AMARANTHINE CHRONICLES BOOK

1

Betrayed By Blood

Dark Revenge

The Final Battle

SHIFTER CLANS SERIES

The Alpha's Daughter

Alpha Ascending

The Alpha's Curse

The Shifter Clans Complete Box Set

TALES OF THE ITHEREAL

Fey Spy

Outcast Fey

Rogue Fey

Hunted Fey

Tales of the Ithereal Complete Box Set

THE FEY GUARDIAN SERIES

Memories Lost

Memories Awakened

Memories Found

The Fey Guardian Complete Series Box Set

THE ARKADIA SAGA

Chosen Avatar

Captive Avatar

Fallen Avatar

The Arkadia Saga Complete Series

ABOUT THE AUTHOR

Tiffany Shand is a writing mentor, professionally trained copy editor and copy writer who has been writing stories for as long as she can remember. Born in East Anglia, Tiffany still lives in the area, constantly guarding her work space from the two cats which she shares her home with.

She began using her pets as a writing inspiration when she was a child, before moving on to write her first novel after successful completion of a creative writing course. Nowadays, Tiffany writes urban fantasy and paranormal romance, as well as nonfiction books for other writers, all available through eBook stores and on her own website.

Tiffany's favourite quote is *'writing is an exploration. You start from nothing and learn as you go'* and it is armed with this that she hopes to be able to help, inspire and mentor many more aspiring authors.

When she has time to unwind, Tiffany enjoys photography, reading, and watching endless box sets. She also loves to get out and visit the vast number of castles and historic houses that England has to offer.

Printed in Great Britain
by Amazon